KNOWN WORLD OMNIBUS

CHAPTERS I-III

LON E. VARNADORE

ACKNOWLEDGMENTS

First I want to thank my dad for helping more than he knows.
And thank Erika for supporting me in ways only she could.

And a special thanks to:
cover design © www.bonobobookcovers.com

CRIMSON PLANET

KNOWN WORLD SERIES

LON E. VARNADORE

CRIMSON PLANET

CHAPTER ONE

The windswept rust tinged plains of Tharsis fell behind Tosh, formally of the House du'Vaul, as his rented saurial mount plodded along the Ancient's Road. The dark green of the domeheaded mount clashed with the red-orange sand of Mars. The wastes that swept outward from the dark Ancient's Road on either side were dry, dreary and deserted. The road they followed was the Ancient's Road, set down and sealed that no sand, nor wind, nor foot, or wagon wheel could damage the dark midnight blue stone path, winding its way from Gods' Home to the Tharsis Crossroads, Lotus, Tharsis Prime, and eventually End Road. The road was a merchant's dream with its well-stocked way stations positioned every fifty leagues and no need to have them maintained, so no road tax or travel tax. The stations themselves stocked by some ancient magi-tech that none in the Mercantile League dared exploit for fear of breaking the wonderful way-station and losing a place to stay. Yet Tosh did fear one thing the road brought.

Bandits.

The ancient foe that harried merchants like Tosh since the invention of commerce. Whether on Earth and using the ancient horse and sword, bow, or firearms; or after the secrets of rockerty and space flight were gained by humans. Space pirates and banditry on other planets became the way of life for those not rich enough to afford the, or the price for using the Guild to travel. Bandits were a constant harassment.

Looking back over his small merchant caravan, the tri-horn behind him bellowed. It made Tosh wary. *What is he bellowing about?* Tosh turned in his saddle to look at the tri-horn pulling the bulk of his cargo. His domehead mount held his personal belongings and a few odds and ends he might have needed for barter if Tosh came across a fellow merchant...or savages of the Southern Martian tribes. The packs on the tri-horn that were tethered to his mount held provisions as well as the bulk of Tosh's trade goods for the southern villages and cities. A cornucopia of farming tools, machine parts, a handful of the lastest entertainment cubes and old fashioned wooden toys. "One never knew what one needed. Customers never do," his uncle and one time head of House Du'Vaul echoed in Tosh's mind. And, the rest of the bulk of the tri-horn cargo was the most precious commodity in the desert climes of Mars.

Water.

Water was held in small jugs and big clay urns that ringed the mammoth beast creating bulges of ceramics. A large tanker was also strapped to the tri-horn, trailing behind the mule-stubborn creature. The tanker also held the four guards that Tosh had paid for with the last of his coin. He *had* to make money on this trip or he would be destitute and his family would disown him. *Well, more like complete the disowning.* Since his uncle's death, when his father took over, Tosh wasn't welcome. This journey was Tosh's one and only chance to prove he could be a merchant like the rest of the men of the family. *And my choices in other personal matters haven't helped.*

He looked up to see the faint light of the Daystar Jove off near the horizon. He had been to Mars many times, usually with his father. The dark red dot on the horizon was an omen, he believed. A sign that he would have success with his endeavors in Tharsis Crossroads. He tried not to look for Deimos, where one of his families manors stood. There would be no help if bandits attacked.

Turning, he looked upon the grim, dark-eyed men and women in piecemeal armor and a hodgepodge of weapons. It was the best Tosh could afford. From Deke whose whole body bristled with hilts of blades to Sophie whose single spear was serpent quick and twice as venomous. The leader of the four sellswords was Isa-Bal-Mu'hal, a near-human from Io if Tosh had to guess. Isa kept himself covered in a dark cloak with hands and feet wrapped in rags to hide his scaly skin. But the large bore long gun he doted over like a babe was intimidating and spoke more than his sibilant speech.

Then, there was Zella.

Zella was from the Northern Tribes, twice as comely as most of any tribeswoman he'd been with before. Bearing the tribal knots of a Darken Tribe; one of the more ruthless tribes of the Northern tribes, he knew that his money was well spent with her around. She glanced at Tosh and for a moment he felt a shiver run down his spine and tried to stop his hand from running over his bearded cheeks. Though her eyes were to far apart, the gun metal grey of her eyes still haunted him from their first meeting in Gods' Home. Tosh had been with many tribesman and women form both hemispheres, yet there was something about her that was intriguing and disquieting. She spoke no more than ten words to him on the trip to the Tharsis Crossroads. He was sure if it wasn't for the coin and the water he provided, she would as likely gut him and taken what she wanted from his corpse than help. She *had* come to his bed on more than one occasion. With his treatments, Tosh made her cry out more than once with pleasure. She was much more of the aggressor than any lover Tosh had had before. Or thought possible. *She's skilled, yet I'll be glad when we part ways.* Zella and her slender sword and dagger had helped with three attacks on the journey South. *I wonder how many more before we reach End Road? Or even before we reach the Crossroads.*

Pushing his thoughts from maudlin and morbid things, he turned back in his saddle to watch the large peach and ochre domes that encased city of The Tharsis Crossroads. Small blue minarets sprouted from the domes at pleasing angles. Supposedly to help the Caliph's Oasis, keeping the moisture and the vegetation lush on the inside of the enormous polished central stone dome. The oasis itself was a place Tosh had been once. He had been with his father. Tosh had learned that it was best to be quiet and not present much a target when he was younger. When Tosh had last been to see the Caliph, his father had tried to sell the youthful Tosh for a few bars of gold. Yet, Tosh's uncle had stepped in to forbid the sale.

Tosh chuckled to push the fear away. "If this deal goes well, I might see the oasis again. And it will be as a friend of the Caliph." Though he heard his father's mocking laugh in the back of his head that burned his cheeks and darkened his mood again. His eyes went to the tattoo gauge on his wrist. The serpent biting its own tail. Three fourths of it was green, menaing he had time before his next injection.

A moment later he heard the blare of a horn used by his guards. He sawed the reins of the domehead to make it stop, the creature stopping after a few more plodding irritated steps. Tosh started to look around, trying to see where the danger was coming from.

The sands shifted on either side of the Ancient's Road, the forms of several bandits in sand cloaks sprang from the ground, crying out in a din of hoots and undulating cries. Most of them held swords or cross-bows; yet the leader, who strode into the path of Tosh and his mount, held an ancient looking pistol of some kind in one hand, a dagger in the other. It looked as though it had been bodged together from at least three different firearms. Tosh heard the whine of the battery from the device. A *raygun? Wonderful...*He didn't trust rayguns and half hoped the thing would blow up in the leader's hand. Tosh didn't want to depend on the flight of fancy for his safety. Tosh kept his hands where they could be seen.

The leader had a strange leather-like mask on, with small bars of bone to protect his mouth. Tosh could only see sun darkened cracked lips of the leader, the rest of his form wrapped in bandages and leathers. The eyes hidden by smoked glass goggles. "Please my friend, do not struggle, don't react poorly." The hodgepodge raygun held on Tosh never waivered as the leader spoke in a charming baritone. "We have come for a few things, nothing more. Give them to us and we will let you go without harm. Sound good?"

Tosh smiled. *Fools.* He turned his head to look at his guards with a grand flourish of his hands. "Why should I, I hired the best—"

He stopped in mid-sentence when his guards dropped off the water wagon, and clasped the hands and slapping the backs' of several raiders, as if greeting lifetime friends after a long absence.

A laugh came from the leader as the tall barbarian Zella strode past Tosh, staring at him with her gun metal cold eyes and stepped behind the leader of the bandits. A small smile pulled at the scar of her face, making the smile look more vicious and cold than Tosh thought possible.

Tosh felt panic sweep over him. Only one word tumbled from his mouth over and over. "What...what...what..."

"You were tricked, my friend. I am sorry," the leader said. "You will live. I swear by my name, Azal Kamir."

"But—"

"It is business," the leader said. The leader then nodded towards Tosh.

He turned a moment to late. A sharp strike from the hilt of one of Deke's sword pommels took Tosh hard, slamming him into unconsciousness.

CHAPTER TWO

Bors let out a yawn as he stretched his arms outwards, arm spanning outward that his fingers brushed the wooden support beams of drinking den. Though the proprietor called it the *Herald Wine Shoppe* it was more a den for any kind of potent drinks for those in Gods Rest. The shoppe had a blue grey haze drifting a foot from the low slung ceiling. The smell of sweat, spice, tabac of a dozen world, beer and sour wine hung in a melange that Bors thought he'd never miss. He took the thick clay mug of Europian white and tossed it back. The sweet and sour liquid helped to shake the fatigue that continued to close in on him.

There was a shifting of the bench to Bor's right. His partner, Rott, was getting restless. "Why are we still here, Bors?" Rott asked, looked up at Bors with a glint in his quick and intense green eyes.

They had been holed up in the *Herlad* for two days waiting and waiting for the Thieves Guild contact. Bors wanted something stronger than wine to help keep him awake. Yet, *kavh* was not in his budget, so he used the horrid sweet and sour Europian white to help prod him awake. He continued to gag the stuff down, which also helped to fight his fatigue. Bors looked down at the tiny Earth Man. "We'd have gone on to Tharsis if you hadn't bungled the last handoff," Bors grumbled at his diminutive partner.

He slapped Rott's pilfering hand from the last of the hard yellow chees they had purchased together with the last of their coin. "We have to lay low for awhile in this shithole." The grumbled turned to a threatening growl at the memory of Rott, bungling handoff of the gems the pair had *liberated* from a caravan merchant lord. The failure burned in Bors' memory and his neck. He took the last crumbs of cheese and licked his fingers clean.

"I wasn't the one who told me to look for a one eyed hag," Rott said, frowning at the lost food. His breath was horrifying and Bors was glad to not have to stare into the chasm of the thief's mouth. It was the reason Bors thought the short man took the name Rott, barely a tooth in his head that wasn't rotting or gone and his breath stank of decaying meat.

"She only had one eye and is a hag," Bors said. *Smelled of witchcraft as well.* He didn't voice this, since Rott would roll his eyes and prattle on about how it was "tech" and not witchcraft. *Witchraft is witchcraft.*

"Bors, because she has gray hair doesn't—"

Bors growled in the back of his throat. *Stupid Earth Man, she smelled of witchery and wickedness.* He didn't see the point arguing with Rott anymore. The Earth Man was a decent sneak theif, yet knew nothing of the horrors in the wild void of planets and eldritch places. *Or event he witchery on Mars*, he made a sign of warding, looking outside the shoppe to see a trace of the red-ornage sand of his native Mars. "Next round is on you." He saw that Rott was just as happy to stop talking about the poor handoff of the gems.

They would need to get rid of them soon, they needed coin to get to Tharsis Prime. Rott said he knew someone there that had a map to some treasure on one of the moons of Jove's Eye. Though the idea of traveling to one of the Jovian moons still caused a shudder through Bors. Space travel wasn't something he could imagine, and the giant metal cocoons Earthmen used stank of strange eldritch things. He did not wish to leave Mars.

A grey skinned Venusian wench swayed her way by, her pale white hair and hourglass form covered by a thin gauzy wrap that did more to accentate her curves than hide them. Her curves and the honeysuckle scent that exuded from her made Bors smile, shaking him of his maudlin thoughts. "Another round for us, please," Bors asked with a leering grin. It had been some time since he'd been in the company of a Venusian, he knew that his love Aliana would understand from her seat in the next world.

The Venusian gave him a sultry look and grin. "Of course, sirs."

Rolling his shoulders out of habit, not feeling the sword on his back made his eyes seek the broad sword. The black iron hilted sword settled against the wall, well within reach of his thick calloused hand, if needed. His finger touched the fetish of a ouroboros and the hint of Aliana's smile fLittlered through his head before he turned away. He looked around the common room, attempting to spot any threats in the smoky haze. A dozen different men and near-men in the varied garb of the Known Worlds settled on benches and seats in ones and twos and one small group of five. Some looked more threatening, some less. None that Rott and he couldn't handle.

Rott wasn't the most trusted, yet Bors trusted Rott's quick and razor sharp daggers, and his greed, to help in any fight that Bors stumble dinto. The group of five looked like a merchant and his guards. Though Bors didn't care what they were. His eyes focused on the fat coin purses of the merchant and the simple guards. He felt his fingers itched. Bors rubbed at his chin and heard Rott cough twice before sidling a little closer. *Either he fancies the merchant or he sees the purse...or both.* Bors chuckled to himself, "Yes, little rat?"

"You thinking what I'm thinking?" Rott asked, smiling up at Bors with a gap toothed smile, ignoring the jibe.

"Probably not, I don't like those kinds of dagger fights like you do," Bors said with a mocking smile at his friend while the serving wench brought him another cup of the wretched Europian white. Rott was handed another tankard of vile fermeted sheep's milk. Bors' nose stung from the pungent smell as it passed close. *It is his vice, as you have yours. Who are you to question his?*

The comely Venusian settled the empty platter down and Bors thought he caught the scent of something a little sweeter in his mug when she handed it to him. She gave him a flash of a wide white smile. *The wine smells sweeter,* Bors mused. *Perhaps she gave ,e something sweeter for a better tip?* He took a deep pull of the drink and was surprised by the sweetness of the contents.

Rott shook his head at what Bors said. "I don't *always* think with my manhood, though it'sss shmarter than yours." Rott smirked back, revealing his rotting and cracked teeth as he slurred.

Bors didn't raise to the jab. "Usual plan?" The barbarian curled his hands, not liking the sudden sense that he *needed* to grab the dirk at his belt. His senses screamed out to stand. "By Von..." he croaked out a half oath before his tongue felt thick and mouth suddenly dry. *Something's wrong.* He tried to say something to Rott. He turned when he heard a *thunk*, seeing Rott's head on the table, the thief snoring.

The last thing he saw was one of the Venusian serving girl coming closer to him, along with two burly types. They smirked looking down at him as he was on the floor and his eyelids closing. One last jolt of energy to try and stand surged through Bors, however his feet didn't respond as they should, causing him to trip over them and slam face first into the dirt floor of the wine shoppe before he blacked out.

CHAPTER THREE

The first moments of waking were rough on Tosh. His brain felt like it was encased in a skull two sizes to small. He reached up to the back of his head feeling the goose egg knot there. It was painful to the touch, causing him to grunt in pain and wince, pulling his hand away attempt to ease pain. It went back to a dull ache at the back of his head which started radiating throughout in body in a series of dull throbbing pulses. Separate from the pain in his head were the dull aches at the wrists and ankles.

Opening his eyes, Tosh realized he was in a prison cell of some kind. Straw and reeds strewn liberally around the floor. The stink of unwashed bodies and human filth gagged him once he recognized the stench tickling his nose and the back of his throat. He attempted to stand and the throbbing on his wrists and ankles grew more painful. Something pulled hard at his wrists while he tried to stand, the realization of what the *clinking* sound was, of thick chains around him stopped him cold. He was a prisoner. Still wearing the clothes when captured, even his wallet was there, though the last few coins and bank notes were gone. Without water or even an eating dagger to help matters.

His mind started to sort through all the possibilities of who had taken him prisoner. His former family was near the top, with his father, Ahmed bin Saldin of House du'Vaul coming to the top again and again.

A new noise caused him to banish the thoughts of his father. The thick chains that encompassed his wrists and dragged at him then disappeared into the dark and dank cell. He realized the chains were moving. *Moving! Someone is in here with me, chained to me. What kind of creature am I bound to!* The images of various cutthroats and vile murders fLittlered through his head as the chains *clinked* and *rattled* louder and louder. And then the form shifted to any of dozens slathering vicious beasts to rend him to bloody ribbons.

Tosh felt bile rise in his throat, looking for a way to escape An icy hand slipped around his heart, squeezing with a constant pressure, causing his breath to come in shallow gasps. *Calm down, you can't panic. It is what* they *would want you to do. Calm down, you can handle yourself.* The chamber was dark and reeked of sweat and some-thing dark and eldritch. Pushing himself into a sitting position, his head aching and his body felt drained. He rubbed his head again, pulling away again from the knot of pain. A moment later, the chains rattled again, a vibration grew in the air until the chains were constantly moving and even starting to pull at Tosh tugging him closer to the thing in the dark. Confused, he looked at the chain around his wrist and at the darkness. Tosh pulled at the chains to stop them from rattling and felt it was attached to something solid. "Hello," he called out tenta-tively, his fear not outweighed by his curiosity to know what was in the cell with him.

"Hello?" Tosh called out again, his voice cracking. He let out a cough, not liking the breaking of his own voice. *Relax, you can talk your way out of anything.* He almost believed himself.

"Stop making noise," a rough, bass voice growled from the dark-ness. The chains *rattled* and *clanked* against the stone ground as they were pulled taunt, and again starting to pull Tosh towards the darkness and the deep human voice.

"Here now, don't—"

"Quiet," the deep voice snapped again, louder and angrier. Tosh *clacked* together. A moment later, Tosh heard the shifting of a large body, knees crackling and chains *rattling* as they shifted up. A mountain of a man strode into the weak light of the cell. Tosh found himself staring up at the seven-foot tall human. *No near-human grows that tall and broad.* The man Tosh was chained too via the two wrist irons and a row of chain links around his chiselled stomach. The mountain of a man was Northern tribe judging from the tattoos and the hair knots. Tosh was guessing since the ink and hair knots were in an ancient and old tangle. He was guessing that he was from an old tribe, or held to some odd tradition. Tosh had never seen someone that tall on Mars, outside of the stories of the ancient Northern tribes of old.

"What...what..."

The giant shook his head. "Bors, you little bird. Please stop tweeting, someone is coming," Bors said, looking at the door and cracking his knuckles and grinning. The giant of a man started towards the door and Tosh had to follow or be dragged along the floor by the chain around his stomach. Tosh elected to walk after the giant instead of traveling across the rough hewn stone on his rump and risking further injury.

When he drew closer, Tosh heard the working of a key in the lock in the door. The door swung outward opening on rusted, hinges squalling in protest. Tosh grunting and covering his eyes as light flooded into the chamber. As did Bors, judging from the low bellow from his right.

A singsong high and cultured voice spoke to them. "Ah, you are both awake, The Master will see you now."

"Who is your master?" Tosh asked, blinking away the pain before opening them again.

Standing before the pair was a Venusian woman, slender and grey skinned, covered in a silk-like robe that flaunted her curves. Her milk-white hair slicked back and hung in a shoulder length queue without a hair out of place. *She is owned by someone who knows the old tradition,* Tosh mused to himself seeing the black and white cords entwined in the queue. Her face was a mask of bored respect. *She had to do this* and wasn't happy about it.

Bors let out a small roar, "Release us woman!" He reached out to grab hold of her.

"Bors," Tosh said, pushing in front of the giant and held up his hands, "Please, let us wait a moment before we give into anger."

"*The Master*, will release you," the servant said in a bored, placid tone. "Please, follow me." She spun on her well made boot heels and walked away.

Tosh caught a strange scent of perfume and spice wafting from the servant. He turned to see Bors reaching out to grab her again. Tosh hissed though his teeth, whispering, "No, Bors, don't. We can try and reason with—"

Not listening to Tosh, the barbarian grabbed at the servant, his hands slamming into a shield that caused multi-hued sparks to sputter from where Bors' hands touched the energy shield. The large man cried out in pain and let out a roar, bringing both arms up in rage.

He stormed forward to make another grab when Tosh shouted, "Stop it, you fool."

Bors turned to look at Tosh, eyes blazing with hatred stared back at him. "Why?" The barbarian bellowed. "Why should I listen to you, Little Bird?"

"Because we can find out what is going on instead of killing everything if we think for a moment! She's wearing a shield, you can't brute force your way through."

"Watch me." Bors' arms twitched and Tosh grabbed ahold of one arm. Chips of pale pale blue ice turned towards Tosh. Tosh felt his bowel turn to water seeing the icy stare. "Bors, we are alive. I am sure there is a reason for this. Let us wait, please. As a bound comrade, we are in the same boat, as it were?"

"Boat?"

"Same land skiff," Tosh said, casting about trying to think of what the Northern might know.

The word calmed Bors. His body still looked ready for violence, yet the giant turned to Tosh and he said, "Very well, Little Bird. We will see if your tweeting will help or hinder us."

The servant hadn't stopped when Bors tried to grab her. Yet she did pause at the end of the long hallway. "The Master hates to be kept waiting. Or damaging his property." She lifted a small golden rod with several jewels in a zigzagging pattern on the two handed rod. She pressed three of the buttons and the irons that Tosh found dragging him down lightened. Bors' eyebrows ached in surprise as he took a step towards her. Tosh only nodded.

"Come along, Bors," Tosh said. "We can't keep *The Master* waiting." There was a touch of sarcasm in his voice that the servant seemed to miss, and even the giant missed it as well. *I have to survive this any way possible. The giant is listening to me, at least for the moment.*

Bors grumbled and stared back at Tosh. Tosh didn't back down, placing his hands on his hips. "They have tech and you have your hands. It won't work."

"It could," Bors said, looking down at the floor his shoulders sagging. He then coughed. "We follow your plan, Litte Bird, *for now*."

Tosh nodded, remembering the angry flare of the barbarian's eyes moments ago. He swallowed and moved forward.

They followed the perfumed servant into a austere chamber of white marble shot through with grey and black veins that throbbed with a pulsing internal energy. Before them, stood a tall thin man in a black mask, his clothes a swirl of grey and black silks that swathed his body, giving him a ragged and mysterious air about him.

The masked face turned towards Tosh and his large brooding companion. "Good you are awake. You will be working for me for a moment. I need you to—"

Bors let out a roar and charged forward, Tosh almost got swept up, yet was able to run forward, trailing the barbarian enough to not get pulled and dragged. "Bors, stop. Stop. *Stop!*" Tosh shouted.

There was an audible *sigh* from the cloth swathed man who threw up a silk-gloved hand. Bors surged forward and struck some unseen force shooting him backwards several feet. Tosh swore he heard the masked man mutter, "Always the hard way, with this one."

Tosh was standing besides the prostrate barbarian, shaking his head as he looked at the masked man. "I told him that—"

"I know, I was there," the man said with a hint of a smile in his voice, flicking his hand and the servant disappeared into a puff of smoke. "I am, *The Master*." His voice filled the chamber and gave a small bow. "I have need of the two of you for a little *job*." There was a titter from behind the mask and Tosh felt his stomach drop. No one that ever laughed like that ever made a straight deal. The disappearance of the servant spoke to the kind of technology The Master had at his beck and call. Tosh had never seen its like before. And, was sure Bors had never seen it either. *Have to be careful.*

"Your father was quiet right to teach you that, Tosh," The Master said. "However, I have made it so you must accept or you and the barbarian here will be put to death." Again the titter of laugher after the cloth covered man spoke caused an itch between Tosh's shoulder blades.

"Why should we work for you?" Bors asked, sitting up and grunting from the pain. He pushed himself to a squat. "Why work for some vile warlock?"

"Bors, I don't think you understand," Tosh said.

"I understand, Little Bird," Bors shouted. "I want *him* to answer the question." Bors thrust a thick finger towards the masked man.

The mask turned to regard Bors for the first time since the barbarian had entered. Tosh saw the eyes of the person behind the mask for the first time. It filled him with dread. No human eyes looked back at him, instead brilliant fluorescent green shone through the two holes of the ebon mask. Tosh knew of no such creature that had eyes like that. At least no living creature he knew of, which was also frightening considering his tutelage and education.

"I can offer you something that your tribe has sought for some time," The Master said. "And, , the reason for your own quest as well. Unless I'm mistaken?"

Bors' eyes narrowed, teeth grating loud enough for Tosh to hear the noise. "You know not—"

"I do and I have it right here." From the interior of the voluminous silks the Master draped upon himself, he pulled out a long slender redwood box. He released it with a slight push towards Bors, Tosh had seen hovering discs used for such a feat, yet never seen a simple box tossed away and moved towards another like this particular box did. Straight towards Bors. There was sudden smell of pine and sandalwood as the box moved past Tosh. It settled to the ground at Bors' feet. The top half opened by itself on a hinge on one side, revealing its contents.

"Do I know what I speak of now, Bors of the Northern Hills?" The smile in the voice was impossible to miss.

Tosh saw a black and pitted iron long sword, very old. He thought he saw what had to be rust and grime clinging to the fuller of the blade in thick clumps of corrosion. The hilt was a dirty mass of leather that looked unclean and foul. The pommel itself was a pale ghostly white orb that made Tosh feel uneasy. "Surely, this is—"

Tosh was silenced by a hard look from the barbarian. Bors knelt before the box, mumbling, "By Von and Hyl…" The rest changed into some garbled antiquated dialect of Martina Tosh had never heard. The barbarian reached forward with quivering fingers, dipping into the box and pulling the sword out and holding it like it was the last relic of his homeland. Though, the look on Bors' borws knit as though afraid it would leap into the air and strike at him like a serpent.

Tosh was shocked. *How can a sword scare* him *of all people*?

Bors took up the sword with more reverence than Tosh thought possible for a barbarian of the Northern Hills. Bors eyes roved over the black-pitted metal with a combination of fear and elation before looking at The Master. "You—"

The masked man held up a single finger of his right gloved hand. "I ask only for a single boon and it is yours."

Bors' shoulder's drooped for a moment before he took a knee, bowed his head, the sword held out before him. "You honor me. *The Soul of the Mother* must be protected. As her bearer, I will do your job as your boon."

"Excellent," the masked man said, his body vibrating with joy. "And for you Tosh?"

The question hung for a moment in Tosh's ears. A single heartbeat pulsed in his chest before he realized what the man's power could possibly give him. Taking in what was before him with Bors and this ancient sword that was somehow beyond precious to the barbarian. *I thought, I thought these creatures were a myth?* "You...you're—"

"The Master," the masked man said with a deeper bow. A small titter of laughter behind the mask causing a sliver of ice to slide its way down Tosh's spine.

"No. You're The Grifter. The one who dangles a tantalizing prize before some fool, only to demands some insane quest of impossibility. There is some hidden price, Bors. You mustn't take the sword."

A light laugh broke out from the Master. "No," he said, taking a long deep sigh before continuing, "I always choose poorly, at least the last two hundred years os so. And, as you can see, I've given the gift to your compatriot. And, I can do the same for you."

"What?" Tosh shouted, not even realizing he had taken a step forward, yet refused to back down. He felt his body shiver with anger. "What could you *possibly* give—"

"I can make sure that your family takes you back. *If* that is what you truly want." The unspoken question in the word "if" set Tosh's teeth on edge.

"Of course it is," Tosh said. *No, there is no way you could...* He stopped himself. After everything he had seen with The Master, could modifying a bit of DNA truly be that out of reach for this creature? "I wish to ask for my boon after this mission."

"Very well," The Master said, giving Tosh a short bow. "For your task, I need you to find the Eye of Saturnalia."

Tosh laughed. "It's a myth."

"I assure you, it is quite real." The voice had a bit more steel in it than before. The man moved closer, his fluorescent eyes pinning Tosh. "Very *very* real."

"There is no such—"

There was a thunderous din, "*It is real!*" The Master's veiled body started to enlarge, growing bigger and bigger grew until he stood ten fifteen, twenty feet tall over the pair. He shouted, enough to buckle Bors and Tosh's knees before driving them to their knee while slapping their hands over their ears to protect their eardrums form the sudden thundering voice. Bors sword fell to the side, forgotten in the moment of the aural attack.

Tosh looked up, his voice trembling while asking, "How are *we* going to find—"

"The Drumgag knows where it is," The Master said with a warm smile in his voice, standing besides Tosh and Bors, his form back to his more human size in the blink of an eye.

"How?"

"You could always try and talk to...*it.*" The masked man raised his hands and Tosh found himself being picked up by an unseen force and deposited on his feet.

"That is insanity," Tosh said, looking at Bors, then The Master, and back. "Why us? We've never—"

"I command power undreamed of, possess knowledge unattainable or matched. Don't question me on this," the hint of steel was back in The Master's voice. "You—"

"Then, get the Eye yourself," Tosh said.

There was a momentary pause from The Master. "I'm—I'm sorry?"

"You are *all powerful* you said. Get the mythological Eye of Saturnalia yourself."

There was a slight titter from the masked man. "Were it *that* easy, mortal, I would. But, it is beyond even my—"

"As I thought," Tosh said, crossing his arms over his chest. "I am done with this maliciousness. I will never—"

"Then, you and your barbarian will die here and now." The Master raised a hand, a dull wan green glow coming from his hand, levelling it at Tosh and Bors. "I will disrupt your very molecules and scatter them across time and space." The bite of steel in his voice was back.

Bors growled, his fists clenching into fists. "*Little Bird* does not *possess* me warlock!" Bors took up the sword, lifting it over his head and surging forward. "You will—"

The Master gave a gesture towards Bors and he was silenced. Tosh, turned to see that the barbarian's lips had vanished. He shook his head. "Bors, you ..." He turned towards The Master. "You are cruel."

"*Very*. But a creature of my word. Find it, and I *will* grant your unspoken boon. And the barbarian continues to be the bearer of *her*."

Tosh looked at the barbarian. Bors held the sword in one hand while touching his face with the other, trying to make some kind of noise, a vague moan came from where the mouth should have been. Bors looked at Tosh, Tosh saw fear, true fear, for the first time since Tosh had met Bors. *I could leave him here, yet what would become of my soul*. Tosh knew when he was beaten and his stance withered. He didn't particularly like the gaint Martian, yet he couldn't abide the cruelty of The Master on another living soul. With a sigh, Tosh nodded. "I will do as you say. Release him."

"That was easy," The Master said with a chuckle. He snapped his fingers and Bors let out a bellow, his lips back as if never gone. The barbarian glared at The Master, Tosh seeing the want and desire to attack the masked man, yet trepidation to do so warred with the giant man.

"I can see I was right in bringing you two together. The charts never lie." The Master let out a self-satisfied sigh and Tosh could practically see the giant smile on the man's hidden face.

There was a flash of indigo, blinding Tosh.

CHAPTER FOUR

Tosh blinked. He and Bors weren't in front of The Master anymore, nor in his hall. Instead they floated in the cold vacuum of space for a heartbeat. The burning cold of the void freezing Tosh's blood, crystalizing sweat on his flesh creating a skin of ice. Tosh felt his breath dragged from him for that heartbeat, his life flash before his eyes.

The next second, he was standing before the stone façade of the outer chamber of a particular merchant lord of Centauri Prime. The home of The Drumgag, a putrid humanoid merchant lord dwelling on Centauri Prime. The pair were billions of miles from where Tosh had been taken and was sure Bors been on Mars as well. For a moment, he felt shaken to the core. *The Master was able to send us spinning billions of miles from one place in the Known Wolrds to another with a flick of his finger? What kind of creature was he?* He felt a cold chill, deeper than the one that struck him a moment ago. *I don't think I want to know the answer.* Most of him was sure he didn't want to know the answer.

There was the titter of laughter from The Master in Tosh's head. "Only trying to help you along…Tosh." The voice of the creature in his head caused Tosh to tremble.

Get out of my head, Grifter.

"Very well," The Master said. "Adieu."

Bors was roaring in outrage, breaking Tosh from the voice from his head. "Where is the *warlock?* I will tear him—"

Tosh put his hand out and touched Bors' side. The barbarian wheeled around. "Little Bird? What is going—where are we?" The crystalline moisture on Tosh's hands cracked and bonded with Bors. When he tried to tug his hand away, the bond of the two icy cold pieces of flesh tore the skin from Tosh's hand.

"Following the plan of a madman," Tosh said, wincing from the pain. " For the moment at least. We have to get that Eye. If we do..." He let the sentence hang, waiting to hear what the barbarian would say.

Bors snorted a moment. "The wizard wasn't smart. We know where he lives. We will return with—"

There was a flash of indigo and Bors' and Tosh's weapons and packs were at their feet. Atop Tosh's was a sleek raygun. A new Quaal Mark 4. Tosh took up the small yet powerful raygun and gaped. Holding the sleek pistol made the reality of where they were and who they were to see solidfy. Not much, but for a scant moment, it helped to make Tosh feel in control. "We have to go in and talk to a loathsome thing. *The Master* is a bit beyond us at the moment." His lip twisted calling him that instead of a few choice words he wished to give the powerful thing. *Not now. Later.*

"Why?" Bors asked. He looked as if he wanted to say more, yet he too bent to gather his kit. Taking great care to pick up his sword, treating it more like a living babe than a weapon.

"Because it is what *The Master* wishes. Let's get it over with, sooner it is done, the sooner we can part ways and go back to our lives as they were before."

Tosh took a look at the outer façade of the giant domed structure of The Drumgag's home. He knew the place well when he had come as child. Tosh was almost sold to The Drumgag for debts his father, Ahmed, had accrued while still under Tosh's uncle. It was only through Ahemd's negotiation that Tosh wasn't sold into bondage. Which still was a wonder that his father had saved him at all. Thought Tosh had tried to repress it, Ahemd had saved him from a rather gruesome fate of being a plaything for the loathsome merchant lord.

Use the one skill he taught you and the boon is as good as yours, the voice of The Master trickled through Tosh's mind. He bit back a reply, turned to look at Bors while thrusting the raygun pistol into the sash of his pants. "Be ready for a smell of horrifying decay and human filth. The Drumgag is…is…not something that can be described. You have to see it. You are my bodyguard, so remain quiet."

Bors gave Tosh a hard look, yet nodded. "If that is what you wish, Little Bird."

Tosh wanted to question the nickname, yet a guard appeared. A barrel of a long arm rifle thrust into Bor's face, a blade of some kind of bone came within a hound's tooth of Tosh's stunned visage.

"Who goes there?" The guard barked. Sallow skinned and skeletal, the guard glared with sickly yellow eyes at Tosh and Bors. He opened his mouth to repeat the question.

"Tosh of the House du'Vaul to see his most gracious and magnificent merchant lord The Drumgag."

Entering the domicile of The Drumgag wasn't difficult once Tosh dropped the name of his House let him in. Tosh wasn't at fault if the guards assumed he was a *representative* of House du'Vaul. *Getting out is going to be the tricky part.*

The gate guard growled something and the massive doors spilt open like a pair of gray stone wings. The moment Tosh turned to look for the guard, he was gone.

A tall and broad shouldered woman rippling with muscles met Tosh and Bors at open maw of a gate, she gave Bors an appraising glance and a wink before looking at Tosh. "Come," she barked in heavily accented Trade Tongue. She wore little except for a rudimentary set of bracers, greaves, girdle, and chest plate. The rest of her exposed body was covered in dark tattoos of black, green and purple. Even her face had splotches of ink and her bald head had several concentric circles growing smaller and smaller the closer to the apex of her skull. Some ink looked old and some looked as though they had been etched in a week ago. When she turned to lead the pair into the stone dome, Tosh saw that all of the tattoos, swirls, whorls, streaks and twisting patterns led to a marking of a stylized "D" in the center of her lower back. It was a brand instead of a tattoo, one that had had some ink etched into the raised and branded flesh..

Bors looked at it strangely and Tosh muttered, "It is how *he* marks those he owns. A grisly shrine of ownership." He had to supress a shiver thinking how close he came to having one of those marks on his own lower back.

Bors growled, yet didn't speak. He gave Tosh a look, then turned to watch for what could be coming, as a good bodyguard would. And remained silent.

As the walked, the stench of unwashed bodies, mold, rotting meat and the cloying stench of to much perfume grew thicker. Bors balked at one point. Covering his face with his hand, trying to ward off the miasma.

Tosh tugged at his elbow a moment. "It is the only way to keep your little rusted sword in your possession," he muttered to the bigger man before continuing forward. "Come along" Tosh said in a tone reserved for servants.

A sudden anger flared in Bors' eyes. He grabbed Tosh by the throat and slammed the smaller man into the gentle curved walls of the tunnel. The inked woman turned and watched, giving a small smile as though she wanted to see how this would climax.

"The Soul of the Mother *is not a rusted sword! It is—*"

"Is there an issue," the inked woman asked, a small quirk of a smile on her inked face while leaning against the wall close to Tosh. She swung her head from Bors to Tosh and back. "I was told to present you two to The Drumgag. Or will I only present one very strong warrior and the mangled remains of a skinny merchant whom angered the man?" There was a light in her eyes at the thought of seeing Tosh's broken body on the stone floor, at least that was how it felt to Tosh. He felt his stomach drop for a moment when Bors didn't answer.

"Unless Little Bird *does thinks* The Soul of the Mother *is* a rusted piece of scrap...no?" Bors asked after a heartbeat.

"No, it is a fine quality sword, magnificent even," Tosh said. Bors dropped Tosh, who smoothed out his tunic and turned to look at the barbarian, tyring not to sound to hoarse. "See here, Bors. You and I are working together. You must take on the role of—"

"Apologize to The Mother," Bors said, sweeping the brittle looking longsword out of the shoulder baldric, pushing the ghostly white pommel to Tosh's face. "Apologize for your insult."

"Who?" Tosh asked. He gave a quick look at the inked woman who seemed fascinated by the sword, but then looked at Tosh and was displeased.

Bors let out a grunt and got Tosh's attention again. "Apologize to Mother."

He's daft. I'm stuck lightyears from home, we are in the den of an unstable power-mad merchant, on a quest of pure insanity and he wants me to apologize *to a sword? By the Makers...*"I'm sorry...Mother." It was his one trick, he did sound convincing.

Bors patted Tosh on the shoulder. Even though it felt light, it still almost drove Tosh to one knee. "We shall continue. Please, lead the way," Bors said, turned to the guide while sheathing his sword.

Tosh took a deep breath and wished he hadn't. The stench that was in the background clawed at his nostrils and bruised throat. "And this is only his antechamber. This will not be easy."

"Why?" Bors asked.

"You'll see."

They entered a large fifty-foot circular room with a twenty-foot circular stone tub in the middle of it. A beautiful pale woman was poised at the edge of the tub, nude save for the fine gold chain and collar around her throat. The chain's length disappeared into the murky water. Her milky skin had a luminous quality from the reflected light from the pool and the floating lantern orbs of the large chamber. Tosh was taken by her in an instant even with her face a mask of bored placidity. Something in her green eyes pulled at Tosh for a moment as she lounged at the edge of the tub. Then, Tosh caught movement beyond her, a bloated lump of flesh that was somehow a deep leathery tan skin. Tosh cringed inwardly, for the creature moved as his eyes set on the creature behind the woman. The thing that they had come to see.

The Drumgag. In the tub was a mound of flesh with small childlike arms and a head that looked more like a bump on a balloon of flesh than a head. The thick putrid flesh mound that was The Drumgag made the bile rise in the back of Tosh's throat. He looked at the coifed blond hair of the creature, it was stylized and shellacked in a way to frame the face into something quasi-human. Tosh felt his hand grip the handle of the raygun in his sash, feeling the hilt bite into his hand from the force of his grip. A sense of dread filled Tosh, overwhelming him for a moment. *This won't work.* "We should run," he whispered to Bors.

Tosh knew that The Drumgag was once human, yet either thought tech sorcery or thorough sheer dumb luck, had existed for more than three centuries, growing into the massive quivering fleshy ball before them with the baby-like arms gimballed and swayed on either side of the massive ball-like creature. All the while, it screamed and bellowed for everything. *Somehow*, The Drumgag become one of the Merchant Lords of Renkashsa, the mercantile center of Centauri Prime and the rest of the Known Worlds.

Bors let out a threatening growl when Tosh's hand moved. Tosh pulled his hand away and ducked his head. "I can't do this."

"Do you want to live, Little Bird?" Bors hissed in Tosh's ear.

Tosh felt the thick paw of Bors rest on his shoulder, gripping him hard enough to pin him without causing pain. "Yes."

"Then, you will do what you were sent here to do." Bors loomed over Tosh for a moment. "I don't to have to kill you, but if I must..."

The barbarian let the threat hang as they were ushed fully into the chamber and the inked woman announced the pair.

"Tosh of House du'Vaul and bodyguard, Bors of the Northern Hills of Mars."

Tosh's eyes moved to the chained beauty that was pulled up towards The Drumgag flopped upon the massive girth of the tub's denizen. She was gorgeous with, porcelain pale skin and blazing red hair. Her eyes a deep jade that when she first turned them to Tosh, he knew that he had to have her, if only to save her from The Drumgag and the vileness of his form and sick perversions Tosh had only heard rumors of. The face her curvy hourglass form pressed against the corpulence of the merchant lord sickened Tosh more than he thought possible. *Focus on getting the gem, save her later.* He felt something loathsome touch his mind for a moment. The overwhelming sense of dread filled him again. He shoved it away, throwing up a mind shield that his uncle Bedrin taught him when dealing with The Drumgag, much like last time.

"You do not let me into your mind?" The Drumgag warbled while drool of a viscous milky white fluid color trickled over his jowls. He slapped at his chin with a small small hand, splattering the viscous fluid everywhere, especially over the nude woman chained and the slick wet putrid floor Tosh and Bors stood upon.

"Why would you need to, oh Great One?" Tosh asked, bowing to keep his eyes from the disgusting tableau before him. *Steady, you can do this.*

"I have great powers and should know what is on your mind. You wish to do business, you open your mind to me," The Drumgag shrieked.

Bors glared at Tosh. "Do it," the barbarian mouthed.

Tosh closed his eyes and peeled back the protection of his mind. He felt the creeping dark psychic fingers of the The Drumgag's mental violation, stroking and probing Tosh's brain, searching for the secrets. Hunting for a reason why Tosh and Bors were there. Tosh felt the mental ooze of The Drumgag burbled its way through his mind. After a few moments the intruding mind pulled away before it reached very far and Tosh was pleased for a moment.

The Drumgag let out a laugh. "Good. I will offer you a thousand credits for your guardian."

"No, we are here for—" Tosh started before being interrupted.

"I want!" The grotesque human blob squalled, throwing his arms out and trying to cross them over his expansive chest, failed and the tiny appendages flailed more, slapping the bulging sides. "He will be *mine*!"

Tosh looked at Bors, who shook his head. "Oh Great Magnificence, my bodyguard is an uncouth barbarian. He barely knows to bow before you as I do."

Bors glared at The Drumgag as Tosh again bowed. "And?" Bors asked, crossing his arms over his chest, glowering. Bors was stubborn, refusing to bow.

Tosh thought he'd have to come up with another lie when The Drumgag nodded with a petulant frown.

"I see what you mean. Though my majordomo would enjoy breaking the man," The Drumgag said as a thin serpent-like man with a sharp widow's peak of coal black hair appeared. The sallow face of the smirking man rang a bell in Tosh's head. He knew the man. *All to well.*

"Setter Mylar?" Tosh asked not able to cover the full shock of his voice.

"It is good to see you again, Tosh du'Vaul." Setter Mylar said with a small bow. "It has been what, five years since Europa?"

"Four and a half. I see you've raised in rank," Tosh said, plastering a smile on his face. He slammed his mind shield down hard, knowing what Setter could do with a few words and the right time to prepare. Europa was years ago, another lifetime. *Setter survived? This is bad.*

"Yes," Setter said, moving closer, a grin stretching his thin sallow face. Though the smile never touched his eyes. He stretched out a slim hand that Tosh had to take if he didn't want to offend the man or his host.

Tosh felt repulsed by the touch of the man. The offered hand was moist and limp. Setter had all the charm of a snake. Yet, Setter was already looking at Bors with a thin lipped smirk. "You would be fun to break," the majordomo said in a sibilant hiss. One of Setter's fingers traced and then tapped Setter's own lips as he contemplated Bors.

Bors glared at Setter, giving the majordomo a small hard smile. "You can try, little man. You will die screaming."

"Bors, show respect. Please," Tosh said, throwing the please-to-not-make-the-large-man-upset-with-him look at Setter. He also shrugged his shoulders. "I cannot be held responsible for what my bodyguard does if angered."

Bors didn't say a word, simply leaning against one of the pillars of the chamber covered with nudes cavorting in ways even Tosh thought were scandalous. He played with a dirk, testing the edge while looking bored before cleaning his fingernails with it.

"Your dog is arrogant, it will turn on its *master* if not...trained properly." Setter said, his head tilting a little while looking at Tosh with the oily smile, eyes that bore into Tosh.

"A risk I am willing to take. Now, I think we should get down to business," Tosh said, trying not to shudder noticeably. "I say we table the talk of selling my bodyguard until you have heard my offer for the Eye of Saturnalia."

Tosh saw that got The Drumgag's attention. The human flesh-ball sat up straighter. "What do you want to know about that?" The bloated creature moved to the edge of its tub, making the redhead gasp and roll to one side to avoid being crushed between the behemoth and the stone lip of the tub.

"I represent someone who wishes to buy it," Tosh lied, though he felt it roll off his tongue with ease. He looked at The Drumgag, yet Setter spoke first. The Drumgag smiling and tried to clap his hands, but simply beat them on his slicked sides with a dull, *thump thump thump.*

"I see. So, why come to my Master?" Setter asked.

"You have the map to it. Or so you claim to—"

"I have!" The Drumgag screeched before Setter could speak. "I have!"

"Then, give it to us," Bors roared from his position, his hands outstretched.

Tosh held his hand up to Bors. *I have to take control of this.* "No, we will—"

"For him," The Drumgag shouted back at Bors, pointing a tiny finger at the mountain of a man.

"No," Tosh said simply. "That isn't going to happen." Tosh shook his head. "I'd be lost without him."

"Then, we are at an impasse," Setter said, shrugging his own shoulders.

"What about a trade?" Tosh asked, trying to take back control of the conversation. He folded his hands to his stomach, keeping them from shaking. "What is it The Great and Magnificent Drumgag wants, *besides* my bodyguard?"

"Riches, gems, power," Setter said as he moved deftly away from the churning tub that his master sat in, some of the reeking water still splashed onto Setter's dark boots. There was a slight frown on the sallow face, yet it was gone before others recognized it.

Not Tosh. He saw it and smiled. "What about guaranteed trade routes on Mars?"

"You have them?" Setter asked looking mildly shocked. The Drumgag loomed over him, drooling more than usual with greed, the creature's fetid breath coming in ragged gasps.

"My family does," Tosh lied. He tried his best not to swallow to hard. *A little lie to get us what we need.* He avoided looking at Bors, already feeling queasy from the little lie. *Wait, why am I—*

He looked at Setter and narrowed his eyes. The majordomo was smirking at him, the near-human's fingers moving in a strange pattern. Tosh realized why he felt the way he did. "Great Drumgag, your major-domo does a great disservice to you. He is using the *Eldritch Ways* to—"

"The Great Drumgag does as he wills," Setter said. "He wishes for me to make sure that *all* merchants and those who come to him are being completely truthful." The pattern shifted and Tosh spotted the hex that Setter was conjuring in front of The Drumgag.

"I do?" The Drumgag asked, confused by the concept of truth from what Tosh knew about the creature.

"Oh great Drumgag, I swear upon your magnificent, your great and lofty mind could weed through any possible lie that a mere mortal like myself could come up with," Tosh said, bowing lower. "I am unable to lie in the presence of one such as you. Your razor sharp wit and keen mind is more than a match for me."

Setter smirked more. "Well, since you aren't—"

"I beseech you, oh great The Drumgag, please remove this man from our talks," Tosh continued forward, shouting at the stinky lump of flesh in the thick dark stained tub. "He is unneeded for this." Tosh put ever ounce of charm into his smile, looking up at The Drumgag with adoration. It roiled his stomach to look at the pinched bump of a head on the bulbous body, yet he *had* to get out of here intact, and with Bors as well. The barbarian was his only protector. *For the moment.*

"Go Setter," The Drumgag said, turning his orange tainted face towards other the near-human. "You aren't needed here anymore."

Setter looked like he wanted to argue. Yet, he snapped his jaws closed with an audible *click*, bowed to The Drumgag while mumbling some platitude. He backed out of the large visting chamber of The Drumgag. His serpent slitted eyes staring at The Drumgag, yet Tosh felt the cold and slimy vision touched on himself as well.

"As I was saying, my great The Drumgag. We need to find the map—"

The Drumgag's small hand reached into the muck of his tub. It's face screwed up in concentration while rooting around in the fetid liquid. He ignored the watery dross spilling out and soaking the beauty that had escaped the muck only to be soaked by the movements of The Drumgag. She let out a small squeak of disgust, yet Tosh knew no matter how vile The Drumgag got, she would stay as his possession. Tosh noticed not a trace of a brand on her pale body, which was very odd. He realized that even though The Drumgag was barely human or human-like, he was still powerful and had immense wealth. She would stay for it, that thought turned Tosh's stomach. *If situations were different, would I have stayed if given the choice?*

The Drumgag pulled out a small box of dark metal, coated in the slop of his tub that beaded, oozed and sloughed off the metallic casing. The creature dropping the muck covered cube into Tosh's outstretched hand. "This has all you need to get to the Crimson Planet. Where are my trade routes?"

"First, we need to—"

"I want the trade routes!" The Drumgag shouted.

"You will have them," Tosh said. He pulled out a small thumbnail sized crystalline oval. He rubbed at the crystal until it started to glow. "I, Tosh Sar Ibn Har du'Vaul of House du'Vaul will sign over all of my trade routes of Mars to The Great Drumgag when I return from the Crimson Planet."

The Drumgag nodded and smiled, one of his hands clasped for the small oval as Tosh set it on the lip of the stone tub. "Is our business—"

"Yes," The Drumgag screeched as he took up the oval of crystal blue. He rubbed it on his flesh, coating it in a thin layer of the fluid of his tub and then dropped it into the tub. "When you return, we talk more." The Drumgag gave a smile, the pulled the redhead to him, kissing and licking her flesh, working towards the woman's face. Tosh saw her eyes flared with rage and disgust, yet her face stayed the same placid mask.

"Let's go, Bors," Tosh said, turning and walking out of the chamber trying to keep his stomach from roiling at the display.

CHAPTER FIVE

When the pair left the main audience chamber of The Drumgag, the first being they Tosh set eyes on was Setter Mylar. The sour faced and tented fingers under his near-human serpent slitted eyes staring intently at the pair. His smirk of triumph confused Tosh until he realized Mylar was flanked by two large men in similar scant armor and body ink like the woman that had led the pair in. "I am *so* glad I was able to catch you before you left." He nodded to one of the two, who produced a small package and offered it to Tosh. "Consider this a gift, in exchange for what you did for me on Europa."

Tosh swallowed hard, staring at the package like it was a viper ready to strike. Yet, he could not refuse such a gift. The Drumgag was the host. His majordomo was an extension of the corpulent creature, and it would be rude to the point of termination of the deal if Tosh didn't take it. "You are to kind, Setter Mylar," Tosh said, bowing his head enough to be polite. It didn't weigh much and Tosh was able to hold it with one hand.

"A lightweight self assembling tent if you find yourself in need of emergency accommodations," Setter said with a greasy oily smile, the grin not touching his serpentine eyes. "It is a fair walk to the main city. I can even have mounts ready for you if you—"

"We'll walk, thank you," Bors said pushing past Setter, unnerving the near-human with a squawk of indignity.

Tosh wanted to say something, yet didn't have time as he followed his traveling companion out the same tunnel that had led to the large corpulent tub dweller. He felt the eyes of Setter on both of them as they left. Once they were at the entrance, Tosh mumbled, "I hate that near-human."

"What?" Bors asked, his head leaning to one side.

"He's a vile—"

"No, what is a near-human?" Bors interrupted.

"Those who are human, yet something that sets them apart. Setter's bloodline played with the DNA, gave him serpentine DNA. His eyes and *other things* mark him as such. The Drumgag isn't completely human, though I have heard nothing to the contrary."

Bors looked at Tosh silently. "Is it a slur?" The barbarian asked, raising an eyebrow.

There was a moment when Tosh wondered if Bors knew about him. He shook it off. *There is no way this barbarian would know about my trials.* "No. It is a label."

"You and the rest of the civilized world have to many labels," Bors said. "You are either a friend, a brother, a sister, elder, or enemy." He ticked off each one on his fingers. "That is all you need."

"Sounds uncomplicated," Tosh said with a sigh.

Bors nodded and shouldered his way through the large stone doors, which opened on noiseless hinges. Once they were outside, Bors plucked the sword from his baldric and cradled it. "I am sorry, *Mother.* The filth cam close to touching you."

Tosh ignored it and took a deep draught of the dry air, free of the putrid stink that was The Drumgag. The weak light of Centauri Prime's only moon, Calbretto, was the only illumination. The dull orange glow on the horizon spoke of the cities of the planet. They were some ways off. Renkashka itself was going to be several days. He was actually thankful to Setter for the tent. He still didn't trust the thing in his hands, yet it was a small comfort.

"Well, what are we going to do?" Bors asked, though his eyes were still on the pitted and rusted sword he held in his hands protectively.

Tosh watched as Bors patted the hilt and pommel and cooed to it like child. *Insantiy. You are stuck together, deal with it.* "We get to a spaceport and find someone who will take us here," Tosh said while hefting the small cube that The Drumgag had given him. It took every ounce of willpower to not fling it away the moment the muck crusted info cube was in his hands. Even after wiping it clean, he still felt there was a stench that clung to the metal form. *The metal can't hold anything, the smell is in your head.* The thought didn't help Tosh feel less disgusted presence by the cube in his hand.

"How do we get to the nearest spaceport?" Bors asked.

Tosh looked over to see the barbarian was still stroking the sword and ignored it. "We could try and walk," he said, pointing towards the horizon and imagined the large towers and rounded domes of the spaceport of Renkashka. "Yet, the road is…Bors, where are you—"

Bors had replaced the sword in its baldric and had started to walk towards the horizon that Tosh pointed at. "You said we walk. So, we walk."

"We could also try and find some other transport. I don't have the sturdy boots for—"

"You will get tougher if you try harder, Little Bird," Bors said, continuing down the road without a backward glance.

Tosh grumbled to himself and started after the barbarian. His eyes went to the small tattoo gauge on his wrist. The red had overtaken half of the tattoo, so he had time before he had to take his next injection. *Damn biology.*

The pair didn't travel more than an hour before Tosh asked for a rest. Bors nodded and without prompting, took the bundle from Tosh and tossed the bundle onto the ground. Tosh was about to ask what he was doing when a large pavilion tent of silver and dark crimson popped up from the bundle, an opening for entrance to the tent unzipped itself as if invitation.

Entering, Tosh was amazed that there were even sleeping spaces for the two of them, rolls of blankets and small pillows, and thin mattresses. Tosh settled on one, Bors settled down next to his, grunting at the mattress, but taking one of the blankets and wrapping it around himself as if checking to see if it would surround his frame. Both were shocked that it did with extra.

"How did you—"

Bors laughed. "I've escorted many on Mars. Soft ones such as yourself use these things. Not complicated."

Tosh blinked at his companion. Hiding his shock, he said, "Interesting, apparently Setter did something nice for us."

"Little Bird, I have been meaning to ask—"

"I have also been meaning to ask. Why do you call me 'Little Bird?'"

Bors grinned. "You tweet and tweet like a bird. And you are smaller than me."

Nodding and then giving a sigh, Tosh dropped into a folding chair that opened when he walked up to it.. "What were you about to ask?"

"What is that cube that the fetid creature gave you?"

"The star map to the Crimson Planet." He withdrew it from his tunic and couldn't hide a sneer looking at it, imagining some unseen slime that had stowed aboard. He touched the middle of it and it unfolded into a large square platter. There was a flicker in the center and moments later a bright explosion of light was around them.

Tosh looked around, his eyes practiced at reading star maps. The images around him were a bit different than he thought, yet he recognized the tri-star system of Centauri. He reached out to touch it and the planet of Centauri Prime. When his finger touched the projection, there was a soft blue hue that the three stars took up and a small bloom of calculations came up. Another bloom of light appeared, to the next system over.

"Halden's Purchase," Tosh said. "But where from there?"

The star map didn't do anything as Tosh touched the new sector of space.

After several seconds passed without a reaction, Tosh groaned and fell back into the chair heavily. "Slag!"

"What?" Bors asked, his mouth half filled with food from the icebox.

"The damn map is a treasure hunting type. It will only give information piece meal. We have to get to the next stop and then open the map again. We can't plan for more than one jump ahead. Gate travel is going to be prohibitive. We'll need a rocket and a good crew."

"I don't like rockets, Little Bird. They smell strange and make eldritch noises."

"Well, we will see what can scourge up when we get to the next city." Tosh grumbled and stared at the new section of space for a moment. *A blood treasure hunt map. The Grifter must be having great fun with this.*

CHAPTER SIX

After two days of dust and one day of blood when Bors having to save them both from a pair of raiders, the two companions arrived in the city of Renkashka. Arriving was a small blessing to Tosh, he felt as though his feet were falling off. He went straight towards the nearest cobbler for a strong pair of boots. He barterde for them with a small toy he had on his person from his small cache of personal affects that *The Grifter* had been kind enough to return as well. The cobbler's daughter loved the way the little automaton capered about and laughed at the jokes the little robot spouted off. The cobbler needed half a day to make Tosh's footwear. Tosh looked to Bors if he wanted boots, yet the barbarian shook his head.

"My feet are tougher than yours, Little Bird. I will manage." The Martian barbarian grinned and waited outside while the cobbler finished up.

The coins from the raiders also helped buy a small meal for the pair and medical treatment for the broken blisters on Tosh's feet. It made Bors laugh.

"Why are you laughing at my pain?" Tosh asked, glaring at Bors.

"You would do better to walk on them, Little Bird. Toughen your—"

"I'll take the boots and the pain meds, thank you," Tosh said with a scowl.

The stink of the spaceport of Renkashka was wretched. Tosh had hated it when he had first arrived in his exile. Five years since and the stench only grew worse. He missed the clean halls and city of Urst and Feld, the major ports that serviced House du'Vaul on Centrauri Prime. *But you aren't there, are you?* "Do you have any idea where we have to go?" Tosh asked Bors, who shrugged.

"What do we do?"

"We need to get to Halden's Purchase, according to the map," Tosh said, indicating the small cube. "Once there, the map reveals the next clue. That means a fast rocket. Or it means attempting to travel through a Gate." Tosh was about to continued, realizing he asked the wrong person and had to explain when Bors spoke up.

"A Gate would be faster," Bors said, then yawned and itched under his armpit.

Tosh stared at Bors for a long moment. "How do you—"

"I am a barbarian from the Northern Plains of Mars, I am not a dullard or stupid. I know of the Gates."

Tosh felt shunned. "But, how—"

Bors rolled his eyes and shook off the question before Tosh could ask it. "Do you have the money or the ability to travel a Gate without a guide?" Bors asked.

"What do you mean?" Tosh asked, realizing he had been distracted. *Better to ask him later about that.* "And how does a barbarian know—"

"Gates have been around for a *long* time, Little Bird," Bors said. "And neither you or I can travel one without a Guild Member, and live to come out the other side...*if* we get that far."

Tosh chaffed at the nickname. "We have some coin from the bandits and the grosteque Drumgag. We could hire a guide to—"

"Where do you need to go, chaps?" A voice piped up from behind the two.

Tosh spun to see a youthful girl, dressed in a bizarre mix of leathers and eye wretching colourful silks. A strange serpent hissed from somewhere before Tosh saw a slender form slithering on her shoulder, raising it's head to get a better look at Tosh and Bors. It spread a strange blue frill on either side of its emerald green scaly head, flicking out a crimson tongue, tasting the air then ducked back into hiding in the young woman's clothing.

"Somewhere pretty far from this dungpile," Bors said, his hand sweeping over the large spires and low flying flitters and skimmers.

"That can be almost anywhere," the girl said with a smirk. She reached up to pet the snake in an absentminded way. The head reappeared, pressing its head into her hand. There was an odd *cooing* noise that came from the serpent, it was unnerving to Tosh.

"We don't have—"

"I can help take you anywhere in the Known Worlds," the girl said, puffing her chest up. "I am a Guildie who can really get around. And I have a special going on as well."

"To Crimson Planet," Bors said.

The sudden jerking of the girl's head made Tosh shake his head, knowing she would balk. "I think you scared her," he said with a sigh. "We should—"

"Not at all, chaps," the girl said, though her voice faltered at first. The creature clinging to her shoulder hissed and its serpentine head slid behind her red hair. She reached up to her shoulder to pet it, then the snake-like creature rub its head against her slender fingers again. "Caught me off guard for a moment is all. I can take you there. Though, it will be a rough one. You sure you're up for it?" She reached up to pet the sides of the creature and rubbed at the underside of the creature's chin as its head poked out the other side of her head, hissing more intently looking at Tosh and Bors. "Quiet Nix. They are friendly...sorta."

"Is your pet upset?" Tosh asked, looking a little amused at the strange creature and already pondering how much he could get for the singular creature.

"Nix is my partner, not my pet," the girl said with a curled lip sneer, eyes narrowing towards Tosh. "Be cautious how you speak of him." She narrowed her eyes a little more at Tosh, "Or what you think of him." There was a hint of a smile in her voice that surprised Tosh.

Oh, that's not good. Tosh nodded, a bit unnerved that the girl looked at him that way. "Well, we still need a guide to...that place. How much will—"

"Two thousand," she said, setting her fists on her hips. "Not a gold piece less."

"No," Bors said. "We will find someone else." He started to turn away from her.

"No one will take you anywhere close to that planet for less than five. I'm giving you a discount," the girl said. "Besides, you won't get much help from the Guild. They hate the place."

"Why?" Bors asked, stopping and looking at her with a sidelong glance.

"Why what?" the girl asked, giving a smile and trying to look innocent.

"The discount and why the Guild won't help?" Tosh asked.

"It will be fun to walk *that* Gate path, in answer to your first. And as to the second, old *old* Guildie law to not go anywhere within lightyears of that particular destination."

Tosh only knew a very little about the paths. There was a memory that the Gate paths could go anywhere, *if* you had a guide. Yet, the Gate Guild were men and women with strange and eldritch ways. She had something of that about her, some strange sense that Tosh couldn't place a finger on. There wasn't a smell or sight or a taste. It was something all encompassing about the Gate Guide. Something that shook him to his core. Something slightly *off* about her.

"Are you ready?" She asked.

"Yes." The both said, nodding in unison.

"My fee?"

"That will be—"

"We can pay you," Bors said. "One moment."

Bors looked at Tosh and nodded towards the cube. "There is no way," he said in a harsh whisper.

"Why do we need it? We have a guide who can take us right there."

"Ah, no. No I can't," Tessa said. "However, I can use that better than *you* can and if could be used—"

Tosh pulled the cube close to his chest. He regretted it since there was still an odor that clung to it that sent his mind spinning back to The Drumgag's lair. The flash of the woman's eyes in Tosh's mind flittered by and he realized that he would have to. "Fine," he said. "However, I wish to keep it in our—"

Bors plucked it from Tosh, who tried to grab it. Then, started to thump at him as he crossed towards Tessa.

Tessa let out a small sigh. "Bors. Please, keep it for now. I will collect it at the end of the journey. Fair?"

Tosh glared at Tessa. There was something that he still didn't trust about her. "Very well. When we reach return here, you will have it."

"Little Bird, that—"

"Its fine," Tessa said. "I accept the conditions and the payment. We should away before we are seen."

Tosh's eye went up hearing Tessa's strange use of language. He opened his mouth to ask when Bors slapped him on the back and said, "Let's go."

CHAPTER SEVEN

With payment secured, Tosh and Bors followed the girl winding her way through the snaking alleys and dismal side streets of Renkaska. Tosh noted that Tessa kept looking up, freezing or hurrying and waving them to stop if they were close to an Observer. They were constructs conjured by some fear monger of a pervious Age from what Tosh remembered. Semi-intelligent as well, for House du'Vaul used them on occasion to keep an eye on the youths of the House. They were about the size of a child's rubber ball, with four to six eye stalks that branched out from the central bulk of the creature. Each stalk ended with in a different colored eye and a massive golden eye in the center of the bulbous creature. Some Observers were used to watch and report back. Some of the constructs possessed augments to their physiology that made their eyes weapons, deadly and silent. The ones in and around the spaceport proper weren't the observation only ones. Tosh witnessed one of the Observers use one of its eye weapons to slay a rook that blundered to close to the floating monstrosity. A bolt of wan greenish yellow streaked from an eyestalk, striking the rook. The wings, then the body slumped towards the streets below. With terrifying speed, the ball of bulbous purple grey flesh lurched and fell onto the corpse, feasting on it with a mouth of razor sharp teeth. The crunching and snapping of bird bones sent slivers of ice through Tosh's veins.

House du'Vaul used them as guardians of the compound on Deimos, It was a stroke of luck and *some* skill that Tosh slipped away from the Observer without alerting the creature or be attacked by one of the little monstrous creations. The ones in the spaceport were thicker, meaner. The singular golden green eye in the center above a thick double row of sharp teeth stained with red rust of old blood, each stalk of the grey purple flesh emerged at various points to twist and afford the thing a 360° view.

"Why are we keeping clear of the things?" Bors asked. "Why not cut them down?"

"The things were sent by the Guild to watch for possible passengers. And, to keep an eye on any Guildie that try and make contact with you," Tessa explained with a great sigh of annoyance.

"Wait, if you are part of the Guild, and these are part of the..." Tosh stopped talking for a moment. "How did you know we were looking for—"

Tess shrugged. "I had a feeling," she said with a forced smile.

"You're lying," Bors said. "I won't—"

"I work, *indirectly*, for The Drumgag," she said, not suppressing a violent shudder. "I was sent to find you and make sure you get to your destination." Nix copied Tessa's shiver moments later.

"He helps us with one hand while he tries to stab us in the back with the other?" Bors asked. "A strange creature."

"Near-Human."

"No, he's *not* human or near-human," Tessa said, looking directly at Tosh. "Trust me on this. He's a vile creature, I wish I'd find something to free me form his influence." She scratched at the head of the creature again as she spoke. The creature burbled and purred as she did. Her shoulders relaxed as she petted the stranger creature more and more.

"What exactly is Nix?" Tosh asked, trying to change the subject as they all lurked around the next corner as an Observer floated closer.

"He's a *vereen*, helps with certain *things* that I run into on the Gate

Path and other people." She gave Tosh a hard smile and turned to wander down the alley that the Observer had left.

Tosh felt his jaw drop. He'd heard of such creatures, but never thought he'd set eyes on one. Rumours where that the Guild used them for their eldrith abilities with the Gates. Tosh gave a nod, strengthening the fact that Tessa was a Guildswoman given how protective of the creature she was. Neither of them very keen on Tosh, he was sure. The *vereen* were prized and desired by the Twelve Families, those who together owned more than ninety per cent of the Known Worlds in some way, shape or form. Even The Drumgag was considered an employee of one of the Families. House du'Vaul would pay good coin for an adult *vereen*. *And a way to get from under my doom.*

Nix turned his frilled bullet shaped head and snarled at Tosh. Small but razor-sharp looking teeth bared in malice while the creature pulled deeper into the folds of Tessa's jacket.

"I don't think he likes me," Tosh said.

Tessa said nothing for a moment, soothing the creature and extended an arm to touch a random ramshackle door. She looked back when she placed her hand on the half rotted wood slats, "You want to sell him. He is against that," Tessa said as she pressed the door open. It swung on rusted hinges with a horrible loud *creak*. "Come on, in here," she said, smling. While looking directed at Bors. It turned to a scowl when she turned to Tosh. "If he *must* enter, he better be careful."

"Why would you take her partner?" Bors asked Tosh, his voice heavy. "I thought you were more honourable than that?"

"You know how much that creature is worth to the right buyer?" Tosh asked, pointing at the retreating form of Tessa. It was a decrepit looking tenement, the smell of dust and old things washed over him as he and Bors drew closer to the entrance.

"Would you give her the money?" Bors asked, eyebrow cocked. When Tosh didn't answer, Bors brushed past Tosh, walking into the rickety building. He muttered something about *"Gost."*

Tosh felt queasy. *Gost* was part of the strange Martian tribes honor code. It was complicated and not something Tosh wanted to get swept up in if he could help it. Yet, he needed the burly bodyguard for a little longer if he was to survive this trip. "Well, of course she'd get a percentage. Yet there'd be expenses and—"

Bors yanked Tosh inside. "Hush, Little Bird."

"I really don't like that nickname," Tosh muttered while yanked into a trash strewn chamber. It was a large single room, piles of paper, books and, strange objects that looked like scientific equipment, or weapons of some ancient culture—*Or both*—dotted the walls and the floor in heaps. Tessa moved around them with surefootedness, even Bors was able to move amongst the piles without disturbing any. The moment Tosh entered, his elbow bumped a pile of papers, he leapt to one side as the paper crashed down about him. Leaping away, right into a leaning tower of books that crashed into discarded dishes with more crashing and banging. Tessa and Bors turned to give him a baleful look while Tosh shrugged his shoulders and gave a helpless smile.

"More of a reason to use it," Tessa said with a mirthful smirk and a twinkle in her eye as she looked at the mess he made.

Tosh looked up and she gave him a smirk. Rolling his eyes, he asked, "Where are we?" He asked, exasperated. Bors walked towards him, ignoring him while closing the door.

"Welcome to my humble abode. And, jumping off point." She gave then both a big grin, holding out both arms and spinning around the room. Her arms flaring outward as the jacket billowed and scarves fluttered about. Even Nix appeared for a moment, gurgling in surprise at the sudden movement of his mistress.

"What? Here?" Tosh asked without even trying to hide his incredulity. Looking at the grubby little hovel of a room. Another door barely twenty paces from where he stood. It was half hidden by a dresser and an upturned frame of a bed. The single chamber was crammed with junk, plus a malodorous smell gave Tosh more reason not to believe the girl that *this* was the place they'd enter a Gate. "You can't be—"

Bors stopped Tosh with a meaty hand, craned his head up with ease. Looking up, Tosh gasped. Twenty feet above him was a thick stone ring, bound to the ceiling by thick coils of brass and copper wire.

A Gate? It had been some time since Tosh laid eyes on a true Gate, since his own house used rockets and only on rare rare occasions was a Gate passage purchase form the Guild. Some he'd heard were mono-lithic structures, sixty feet or more across. Some even bigger, one was rumoured to hide in the Asteroid Belt of the Sol system between Mars and the daystar Jove. *This can't be a Gate.* "It's so small." *How can this be a—*

If it *was* a Gate, it was closed. The miasma of the room made more sense to Tosh while he looked at the stone ring. All Gates had a strong odor of age and dust. "You use the Path from here?" Tosh asked, still not fully believing it.

She nodded, smiling up at the stone ring. "Only place I really care or want to go to or from. The sanctioned places are under stricter Guild control." She looked back at Tosh, rolling her eyes. "Besides they are to *Tuesday* for me, know what I mean?"

"Aren't all Gates marked and regulated?" Tosh asked, ignoring the random comment.

"Usually," Tessa said with an off-putting smile. "This one is a bit of a rogue, she is. Not truly on the books of the Guild." Craning her neck up she said, more to the ring then to anyone else, "Isn't that right, girl?"

An odd thrum echoed throughout the room as if in answer. Tessa nodded as if it were a response she expected.

Tosh took a deep breath to relax himself. "So, you are an *unsanc-tioned* Guildsman, using a *rogue* Gate? No wonder you would agree to take us to the Crimson Planet for such a discount," Tosh groaned. After a second, he nodded, "We should leave, Bors."

"Why?" Bors asked. "What is wrong with it? And what does 'to Tuesday' mean?'"

Tosh sighed. "She can't do normal missions. She does dangerous ones," Tosh responded. "And she's a Guildie, they always say odd words, Bors or act bizarre."

"To survive, I have to do dangerous missions," she said with a shrug. She looked up at the Gate. "Besides, *this* Gate likes me more than the other Guildies. She and I sync up well. And Tuesday is that day of the week that really sucks, you know? You only just started the work week, hump day isn't until tomorrow. The weekend is forever away. It's all boring *business* and its a *draaag*, you knowhatImean?" Her last few words came out in a rush. She started to move around the room, taking up a knapsack and putting a book inside, then a packet of food wrapped in a silver foil. She then took it out, peeled it open and started to munch on the dark brown cube of food. All the while, she roamed around the room, humming a tuneless little ditty to herself picking around the room, searching for something.

Tosh and Bors stared at each other for a minute. Then at Tessa. *We've made a terrible mistake,* Tosh realized. He thought Bors had come to same conclusion when Bors started to roar with laughter.

He looked at Tessa and laughed harder. "I like this one! By Von, you're funny!" He wiped at his eyes. "We made a good bargain, Little Bird."

Tosh let out a groan, his head starting to hurt. *Surrounded by madmen, wonderful. I'm doomed more than before.*

Tessa's head snapped over to the door.

The door that Tosh stood in front of bowed inward with a shuddering series of bangings. Tosh jerked away while Bors already stepped towards the door, pulling his short hafted notched axe from his belt. His jaw clenched when his free hand went to the dull white stone pommeled long sword across his back before his hand came away from the sword hilt. "No room," Tosh heard Bors growl, more ot himself than anyone else. He pushed himself in front of Tosh.

A loud voice bellowed from behind the door. "Guildsman Tessa DeLillo, you are in violation of—"

The rest was lost in a rushing of air and wind. Tosh turned his head to see Tessa standing on her tiptoes, her arms reaching upwards while her eyes rolled back to show only the whites of her eyes. Screwing his head upwards to witness a liquid layer forming along the now open center of the Gate. Rippling and stretching, the layer of liquid was drawn down towards Tessa's outstretched hand. She extended her other hand towards Tosh. He reached out, but she shifted her hand to point more towards the door. "Down!" She shouted at Tosh.

Tosh was shoved to the ground by Bors. He was glad the barbarian did when a violent boom a moment later reverberating in Tosh's ears. He peaked out form behind his hands. The liquid coalesced around Tessa's pointed finger, blasting from her again, striking the door. Tosh peaked over the beefy shoulder of Bors to see that whatever was on the other side of the door was obliterated. Taken in the blast that destroyed the door. A perfect symmetrical hole four feet across had punched through the dilapidated door and bits of the walls. A bloody echoing *splat* drifted into the room. Standing up, Tosh could see the other side of the door. Catching the sight of two forms in the remnants of black uniform of Guildsmen. Both of them cored by whatever had destroyed the door as they fell to the ground with a wet *splat* of blood and viscera.

A moment later, there was a squall of howling winds, screaming, and an intense cold pain stabbed into Tosh's limbs. Blinking, Tosh realized they were no longer on the floor of the dilapidated flophouse of Renkashka. They were he sprawled on a lush bed of grass and loam. Bors was still atop of him. Tosh tried pushing the barbarian off. Bors leapt to his feet, his long blade clearing his scabbard while his dark green eyes sought a target to attack.

Where are we? Disoriented and woozy, Tosh tried to rise. He only managed to lift himself onto his hands and knees feeling even sicker. A moment later, Tosh felt bile rise to his throat and vomitted up the last few days worth of meals. Finishing with a soft groan, he tried to push himself onto his feet. Weakened by whatever caused the shift in his reality, he only succeeded in rolling away from the puke because of a small hill he was on and rolled down the hill a little before being stopped by a rock.

Never thought I'd go through something like that. He'd experienced Gate travel before. Never so erratic or intense. *Is this what she meant by dangerous?* He tried to speak, only to let out another groan of pain. Bors dropped a skin of water to Tosh, the barbarian's eyes never looking away from the his search to find something to attack. Tosh grabbed up the skin and started to greedily suck at the water.

"What was that?" Bors shouted, turning to look everywhere at once.

"That was a Gate Transit," Tessa said, sitting on the ground a few feet from them, petting Nix, sitting with her legs crossed in front of her. The creature was cradled in her arms like a baby. Tosh could see the full extent of the creature. It looked like a thing out of myth. What he thought at first was a small scaled snake-like creature of red scales with blue frills was more. A serpentine head and slender body with a pair of gossamer thin insect-like wings a third of the way down from the head. Its coloring was a dark crimson that faded to a pale ochre near the tail, which ended in a viscous looking stinger.

Tessa scratched the chin of Nix again and then let the creature spring from her, letting it flitter about around her hands and her body. She let out an innocent giggle and clapped her hands as Nix moved in wider and wider arcs around her.

Tosh looked up to see the light of the star was much like Sol, yet farther away. The grassy knoll he found himself on was much like that of Earth. Though by moving a little, it felt more like Martian gravity.

"Where are we?" Bors asked. There was something in his voice, a catch that made Tosh turn to look at his bodyguard.

"*When* is a better question," Tessa said, smiling up at the little flying serpent. She scratched under the beast's chin when Nix dipped down letting Tessa's fingers scratch away. Nix burbled and gurgled like a baby, getting attention from a doting mother before flittering away again.

"What do you mean *when*?" Bors asked, looking at Tessa with a mixture of fear and anger.

Tessa looked at Tosh, her eyes seeking help. Tosh only shrugged. "You'd better explain," Tosh said. "I flunked that part of Uni."

"Do you know how the Gates work?" Tessa asked Bors.

"You walk in and you walk out somewhere else. Teleportation," Bors said.

"Something akin that. But, space and time are rather...*fluid*," she said, placing her hands together, palm to palm, before interlacing her fingers. It was a very exact and precise movement that caught Tosh's eye. He'd seen it before at Uni and never understood it when the Guildie tried to explain the "science" of the Gate.

"Huh?" Bors asked, clearly confused.

"You can go into a Gate and come back to the same spot, but in a different time," Tessa said.

"Are we on Renkeshka?" Bors asked.

"No. I had to go somewhere and somewhen else. And, *She* touched both your minds for a safe place. Well…safe-ish."

"She?" Both Tosh and Bors blurted out, looking at each other.

Tessa pointed up. Tosh's eyes followed Tessa's gesture. After a few moments, he was ready to write Tessa's actions as being a strange Guildie. He then saw it. A faint outline about twenty feet from where they were on the knoll. It was hard to make out, but after staring hard at it, the outline grew sharper. *It's a Gate. It hasn't moved. Wait, are we—*

"Then, we are on Mars?" Both Bors and Tosh asked, looking at each other when they realized it was at the same time. Both then looked around the odd landscape that wasn't Mars, yet was.

"Yes," Tessa said with a simple nod.

"When?" Bors asked, looking around. Seeing something, he plunged his sword into the ground, dropping to one knee with his head bowed.

Tosh looked at where the barbarian was looking at and saw a large mountain, a *very* large mountain, taking up most of the view of the North. "Is that—"

"Olympus Mons, before it was destroyed," Tessa said with a nod of her head.

"So we are in the far flung past," Tosh said, doing some math in his head.

"Ancestors be praised," Bors said. He started to mutter something in his native tongue. Something that was to fast for Tosh to completely comprehend. He caught something about the *Mother* and something about being the right bearer of the *Soul*. Yet most of it was gibberish to him. Bors continued to touch the pommel and Tosh thought there was a glow coming from the white gem. He banished it from his mind as a trick of the light.

"And now?" Tosh asked. "Are we at a waypoint or are we going somewhere soon?"

"A bit of both," Tessa said, giving the serpent another scratch under the chin as it darted around her. She let out a small tinkling laugh and Nix started to swirling higher and higher in the sky, looping and bending his body into different shapes, flowing from one to the next in an endless string of red scales.

"Care to elaborate?" Tosh asked.

"Let him finish his prayer. I can replenish and then we can go." Tessa called Nix to her lap, she then leaned on her arms back and took in the sunlight. She let out a sigh, looking up at the light with a wistful smile on her face. "Always a great place to replenish."

"Replenish?"

"It takes willpower, concentration, and a bit of luck to use a Gate," Tessa said, not even opening her eyes. "*She* is a bit greedy, but worth it." Tess turned her face further up, eyes opening to look at something in the sky.

"We are on ancient Mars, Tosh," Tessa said without moving or opening her eyes. "Not all Gates are as tethered as *She* is to me. *She* needs to recouperate as well. That blast of energy to distract those *Tuesday* Guildies took more out of her than I thought. Won't be able to leave here for several days. So, rest up." Tessa then let out a sigh. She drifted off to sleep, softly snoring. Nix fluttered down onto her chest, curling into a tight coil, gave Tosh one final hiss of derision, then tucked his head into the coil he made and started to sleep.

Tosh looked over at Bors and thought he'd be at it for a time. Sighing, he stood, found his legs weren't as shaky and walked to other side of the knoll. "Don't go to far," the words of Tessa came as Tosh walked down the other side of the knoll.

"Understood," Tosh said. He settled into the knee high grass a few dozen feet from the crown of the knoll and took in the sights of ancient Mars. There was much to it that he thought was amazing. The landscape was painted with a dozen different greens. Forest, emerald, wan yellowish green, lime and even olive. Each shade of green on some soft rolling hills except for the giant colossus of Olympus Mons behind him. *A peaceful place here.* He took a deep breath and felt something thrum on his wrist. He looked down and realised the tattooed snakes scales were pure red.

"Wonderful, time for another shot." He abhorred the needle, yet he had chosen to go down this path. Luckily the injector was mostly painless. He pulled it from a fold in his robe and injected it into his arm. The hormones would take some time to continue to block what they needed to. Knowing it would take a full year to complete was an annoyance. At least he was close to what he truly desired. And with the boon that was promised by The Master, he would be able to afford what he needed for years. And still have enough to live comfortably for a long long time. He closed his eyes and let himself relax. The sun and warm breeze started to lull him to sleep. He hadn't realized he had fallen onto his back, yet it was so nice and soft that he ignored it. A warmth suffused Tosh which let the tension start to ease more and more. His mind reaching out to the dream of the future, it made him smile. No need for injections.

He would be whole. *Such a wonderful dream...*

CHAPTER EIGHT

Bors took in a deep draught of breath before finishing his prayer to the Mother Mountain. His felt blessed to witness the grandeur of her former glory. *It is truly a spectacle to witness Her as She was.*

A soft susurrus of words trickled into his head. *Thank you, Bors of the Hidden Mountain. You've done a great service as my bearer.*

"I'm not worthy," he replied, his words a whisper of True Martian tongue. "I—"

I would be unable to be moved if you weren't worthy, my child. As if to give an example, the sword trebled in weight, Bors arms felt wrenched from the sudden weight that drove the sword point deep into the Martian grass and soil. It then changed to its normal weight in an instant.

"Thank you Mother." He stood, feeling a new confidence buoy him. He looked around for the rest of his party. Though his eyes went to the majesty of Olympus Mons again and again, still disoriented by the sight of it. Finally, he sought Little Bird and the shaman. He saw the Little Bird, where he had been before he started the ritual. Yet, the shaman was hovering over him with her dragon perched on her shoulder. She turned her face to Bors and she looked stricken.

Bors bounded forward towards his charge and the shaman. "Bors," came the voice of Tessa, tinged with fear. It made Bors turn to see her waving towards him. "I think something is wrong with Tosh."

"Little Bird?" Bors asked, looking down at the prone form of his charge. He reached out to touch the sleeping man when Tessa stopped him with a violent slap to his thick calloused hand.

"Stop, don't touch him," she shouted, eyes going wide.

"Why?" Bors looked at his charge and noticed a pallor starting to grow from one side of his face to the other. "What is going on?" One hand wrapped around the old hilt of *Mother* as he looked down.

"Damn it, I told him to be careful," Tessa said, planting her hands on her hips. "Damn fool." Her dragon growled and hissed at the inert form of Little Bird.

"What's wrong, shaman?" Bors asked, looking at her.

She looked at him, pulled up short by the remark "I am not a shaman. I..." She stopped when she said this, looking at Bors. "Maybe I am to you." She nodded to herself and then at her dragon companion.

"You have a dragon, that means you are a shaman of some power," he said. He had not known a single wise woman or shaman of the Martian tribes to have a *dragon*.

"I am not, but that isn't important," she said, waving her hand at Tosh. "What *is* is that he is on the burrow of a soul eater. It has already started and Tosh can't wake up, or he'll be without a soul."

"How do we save him?" Bors asked, feeling a sickening plunge in the pit of his stomach. *I've already failed as a guardian.* As he watched, the shaman revealed a pale tentacle sliding along Little Bird's side. The flesh of Little Bird paling as the tentacle caressed the skin.

"How do you feel about battling something in his mind?" Tessa asked. He turned to see her biting her lip, eyes flickering back and forth from Little Bird to Bors and back.

Bors clutched the hilt of his sword a little harder. "The Soul of the Mother is with me, I will—"

"No, it won't be real...never mind." She reached out to take his hand. "It is strange, usually the soul eaters of this place go after women. Rarely do they attack men."

Bors thought better than to say anything. It wasn't his place to reveal anything about Tosh. Bors knew what Little Bird was, yet Tosh was Bors' charge as well and that came with a certain amount of respect to privacy.

"What do I—"

Before he could finish, Tessa snapped a hand up her first two fingers tapping the center of his forehead above his eyes. He felt his body grow heavier and heavier. He tried not to fall to one knee, yet he felt himself yanked downward. His eyes closed. Whis knee hit the ground, it wasn't the soft loam of ancient Mars that was. It was hard packed clay titles of ochre color.

He looked around, finding himself in a lavish tiled and wide hall-way. It wasn't like *The Master* or the one of the vile creature The Drumgag. He saw a young girl turned her face from Bors as she following a man in dark red silks. She had on a snowy white silk robe.

Bors spoke with hesitation, "Little Bird?"

The girl turned her head, a long black banner of hair swirling as she did. "Who are you?" She asked, her face confused for a moment. She turned back, saying over her shoulder, "Come on, we have to stay close to father."

Bors stood up, following. The voice was more childlike nor stub-ble. He felt as though something was finally put in place with Tosh and who he was. She was. *It explains much.*

"Toshlynn, attend!" The thunderous shout of Tosh's father snapped both Tosh and Bors to the tall robed form. He had turned to see Tosh had fallen behind. His eyes blazed with a dark fury.

Tosh scurried toward her father, head ducking low and apologizing. "I'm sorry, father. I—"

"You are a weak thing, I understand," her father said, touching the child Tosh on the shoulder. "You can't help what you were born as."

Bors stepped forward, blinking and he saw Tosh as Bors had met him in the prison. Taller, lean and with a hint of stubble on his face. The banner of black hair gone, cropped short, head bowed with shoul-der's slumped at the words of the man before Tosh. "I am sorry, father." This time,t he words sounded more like the words of Tosh that Bors knew.

"Tosh, that isn't your father," Bors said, moving closer and witnessed the image of Tosh's father growing more and more nebulous. He drew *Mother's Soul*. He felt a veil dropped from his vision to see a huge wormlike creature, wispy tendrils connecting to Tosh who looked at Bors. He looked like a marionette, unable to move on his own.

"Bors, why are you drawing your weapon. This is my father."

"Your father thinks you weak?"

"Yes!" Tosh screamed. "He always thought I was weak. Always thought I was *wrong*. I'm a weak man, never comfortable with what I was. Even though I knew was given the wrong form."

"Tosh, you're—"

"You aren't right, *girl*!" The voice of Tosh's father reverberated through the ochre hallway. "You're a *freak*. You should give in—"

"No!" Tosh shouted, sinking down to his knees before the creature.

Bors reached forward to help Tosh pull back further from the towering wormlike thing. "You're not weak," Bors hacked at a tentacle slithering towards him. "Tell him."

"You're wrong. I'm not weak." Tosh looked at Bors. Then turned and said it again, with more strength, "I'm not weak! You're wrong."

Bors moved closer, reaching out to grip Tosh by the shoulder. "You aren't. You are more clever that I. Tell him."

Tosh turned to the creature. "I am a man, father. I am not weak."

With an unnaturally loud keen the creature's wispy tendrils pulled away from Tosh.

"We are leaving," Tosh said. He took a step away from the creature. It roared and plunged towards the two. Bors stepped in front, slamming *Mother's Soul* up into the creature. The blade bit deep into the creature's translucent flesh, pale blood, little more than water, erupted from the creature as Bors stood in front of Tosh, shielding his charge. He held the stance until the wormlike creature was still, dropping to the floor of the hallway in two sections. As the creature dropped, the hallway grew more indistinct and fuzzy.

Bors turned to see Tosh was covered in the oozing muck of the creature's blood. "Thanks," Tosh said, wiping the ooze from his face and shoulders. "Couldn't have tried something less messy?"

"I saved you," Bors said with a chuckle. "Don't be such a preening bird."

Tosh smiled back and smiled. "Thank you, Bors."

"You're welcome," Bors said, smiling at the thrill of combat still sang in his blood. He gripped the *Soul of the Mother* and told her in his head that it was enough. There was resistance, yet he felt the sword yield. "We should leave."

"How?" Tosh asked. Looking around the hallway grew hazy and indistinct, yet they remained.

"I have no idea."

There was a jolt and Bors felt himself rocked to his knees. He blinked and saw Tosh on the ground, groaning.

"What was that?" Tosh asked, gripping his head.

"That was a mistake," Tessa said. "I told you to be careful."

Bors was about to rise up when something struck him in the back of the head. The last thing he heard was Tessa screaming and Nix letting out a growl and hiss before Bors was unconscious.

CHAPTER NINE

B ors came to, looking at the sky. His wrists and ankles hurt. He found that he was tied to a pole made of some kind of metal. He was carried like a prized hunt trophy. He heard the mumbling of Tosh Little Bird was in front of Bors. Bors looked around to see an ancient enemy, long since thought to have died out.

Green skinned and bipedal, snarling and grinning with the malign cunning of their race. Saurials. Lizard-like creatures of Mars, the four arms abominations that had died out well before Bors was born. His head was a little fuzzy from the blow to the back of his head, for a moment, he wasn't sure how he had gotten here. Then, he remembered the scream of Tessa. "The Hazak! Do not fear Tosh. They are taking us to be eaten."

"How can I *not* worry with that kind of information?" Tosh cried from in front of Bors.

Bors let out a small laugh. "I will save us." Already, Bors worked at the thong that held him. Yet, a Hazak stabbed at his arm to make him stop. It growled at him in a perverted form of the True Martian tongue. Yet, Bors knew that he had to bide his time.

"How?"

"Working on—"

The same Hazak growled, "No talking," as it stabbed Bors in the side again. The creature laughed with the cruelty. Bors used the pain to fuel the simmering rage, feeling the rage the *Soul of the Mother* had ignited in him with the battle of the Soul Eater.

With a roar, he yanked hard on the thong. The pain of the thing biting into his wrists helped to add to his rage and pain, the blood helped him to slip loose of the bond. The Hazak tried to jab at Bors, yet the barbarian grabbed the haft of the spear and pulled it hard. The Saurial was not ready for it and the spear flew from his hand. Bors used the metal tip to cut his legs free first, the dragged down the pole he was attached to, throwing the raid party into disarray. His vision turned red as he attacked the murderous Hazak.

In the midst of the rage, he found the *Soul of the Mother* and the singing of rage and the blood pounded in his ears. When he came to, he found himself alone with Tosh, both covered in the dark blood of the Saurials. Tosh looked a little shocked by what happened, and Bors felt a sudden queasy feeling. "Tosh, are you—"

"No. I'm not. Nothing about this has gone right from the start. I should be in Crossroads, drinking and trying to make a name for myself. Instead, I'm some time in the past, I am filthy, and on an insane quest for something that is a myth!"

Bors let Tosh shout and rant a bit more. When he finally stopped, Bors slapped him on the shoulder. "Done?"

"Going to say I was being hysterical and a woman?"

"No," Bors said with a shake of his head. "You're a soft person who has never had to deal with these things. But, this is not some romance. You will have to get your hands dirty. We should try and find Tessa."

"Did she get captured?"

"I doubt someone like her could easily get captured."

Bors instructed Tosh to keep an eye out while he scavaneged for anything from the Hazak that they could use to get back to Tessa. As he did, he found a small bag the leader of the raiding party had. Bors dug through it and found something strange. It was a small roll of ivory that was a scroll case.

Pulling it open, he found a small rolled up piece of parchment. The message was short and to the point. And it made Bors' blood run cold.

"Kill the robed pretending to be a male. And, her bodyguard. You'll be rewarded." It was signed Ibn du'Vaul.

The name of Tosh's House? His father? Who else would still call Tosh "her." It wasn't Bors' place to call Tosh anything but a man. He knew others who thought themselves born in the wrong gender. *He can't know.* Bors ripped the note to shreds and dropped them into the cooling pools of blood. The pieces of parchment soaked up the crimson fluid and were indescipherable.

If I tell him assassin's are after him, he'll believe me. No need to tell him who sent them...for the moment.

————

The pair crested a rise an hour later, the grass becoming a bit lusher like what Bors remembered. He shaded his eyes and dropped to the ground, pulling Tosh down as a bolt from a raygun shot through where Tosh's head was a moment before.

"Who is—"

"Saurials," Bors said as he pushed Tosh backwards, creeping backwards below the top of the rise. He saw the two beastial men moving towards the rise and sighed. "It seems that they wish for a frontal assault."

"What are you going to do?"

"Protect you," Bors said. He gripped the hilt of Soul of the Mother and felt the desire to kill welling up inside of him more than before. Seeing that Tosh was safe, Bors waited half a heartbeat more and then stood, seeing that the two Saurials were closer than he anticpated. He felt a primal scream tear into the Maritan air and he ran full tilt at the two adversaries. The scream stunned the two for a moment, enough for Bors to reach a distance where the rayguns would be harder to weild.

Charging full tilt towards the Saurial that wielded ray guns, Bors was struck in the arm by one red ray, the other going wide. In the moment, he sliced down his long blade across in a wide arcing slash cutting down both Saurials in one cleave. The smaller one losing his head in the savage cut. Bors looked down at the remains of the two, his right arm throbbing in pain from the burn of the ray. He looked at his charge and grumbled, "Its safe."

"I figured it was safe after the blood splatter," Tosh said, wiping at a small spot of blood on his cheek.

Bors shook his head. *Why the Makers decided to cast my lot in with this one...*

"You chose this, bearer," the voice in his head said.

I know.

"Then, press forward. And I must feed."

He looked back at Tosh. "I don't like this." He tried to keep Tosh distracted as he "dropped" his sword point into the felled Saurial. He was disgusted that the *Soul of the Mother* needed to drink blood, yet she was more than a sword. And he was her bearer, not her elder.

"What isn't to like? We have sand and grass? We have...more sand and grass...it's a paradise," Tosh said with a sneer.

Bors let out a sigh. "This job is to dangerous for us both."

"And?" Tosh asked, looking at Bors with a sour look.

Bors pointedly looked Tosh up and down. "You will not survive."

"That's why you're around," Tosh said. "You're here to help keep me alive." Tosh placed his hands on his hips. "That was *The Grifter* put us together for his little treasure hunt."

Bors shook his head. *Time to end this farce.* "Listen girl, you—"

"I'm a man," Tosh said, trying to deepen his voice. "You, yourself—"

"I don't care. But, you weren't born a man," Bors said.

Tosh was silent. Finally, in a voice close to cracking, he asked, "How did you know?"

"Your scent," Bors said, touching the side of his nose. "There was something different about you. And whatever happened with the Soul Eater. I saw what you were.""

"So, you think I'm to weak? That because I was born female—"

Bors shook his head. "By Von, no. No. It is to dangerous since these damn *Hazak* sent assassins after us and I can't watch my back and yours from the normal dangers *and* assassins."

"How do you know that—"

"It is what I would do.' Bors said nothing of the letter found in the pack of one of them, *Better to leave that until we are safe...safer.*

The two were quiet for a moment. Tosh leaned against the wall. "I prefer to be referred to as a man."

Bors nodded. He had known others of his tribe that preferred a different gender. It wasn't like the *civilized* world. There was some hang-ups that he could never understand that more *civilized* ones believed. "One of my best friends was born male and preferred to be treated like a woman, Dala."

Tosh's eyes narrowed. "Did she take anything?"

"There are herbs and draughts. It wouldn't be impossible for the shaman's to help one these changes along. They 'knew-of-the-Old-Ways,' say the shaman."

"Did the tribe care?" Tosh asked, a little sheepishly, not wanting to look Bors in the face.

"The tribe cared about the tribe. As long as Dala pulled her weight doing what she was told to do, she was part of the tribe."

Tosh gave a small laugh. "Sounds like the tribe is a bit better than some of the Known Worlds."

Bors shrugged. "Doubtful. There are places for all people, Tosh. You think you're a man. Then, you will be treated like one." Bors took the sword that he hadn't cleaned yet and wiped some of the cooling congealing green blood from it with his thumb. "Come closer."

Tosh looked at him, sneering at him. "Why? You're going to make me lick it or something?"

"Do it," Bors said, a bit more sternly. Tosh moved forward. Bors touched Tosh's high forehead and dragged his fingers over to the right, then back to the center then, to the left then down the bridge of Tosh's nose to make a "T". "You anare now honorary tribe of the Hidden Hills. Welcome."

"What was that for?" Tosh asked, his hand not quite touching the blood on his forehead, his voice tight. Bors assumed he was disgusted by what had happened.

"You are now tribe. Now, I will protect you as tribe," Bors said with a smile.

"You weren't before?"

"No."

"Why?"

Bors gave a chuckle. "Tribe and protecting a person from being stupid are different things. I get paid one way or the other if you die. If you die as tribe, because of something I did or didn't do? That is indefensible." Bors touched Tosh's shoulder. "Understand, brother?" He asked with a reassuring squeeze of Tosh's shoulder.

Tosh raised an eyebrow. "I'm your brother now?" He sounded surprised.

"All members of tribe are brother or sister. Or elder." Bors said with a big grin.

"Sounds uncomplicated," Tosh said with a small smile, looking away.

"It is," Bors said. After cleaning the blood off, he sheathed *Mother's Soul*. "Are you ready to go find Tessa?"

Tosh gripped the raygun tighter. "Yes."

CHAPTER TEN

"This is where you two are? Playing with creature's blood? That's a bit, *weird* isn't it?"

Tosh turned to see Tessa stepping out from behind a small rock pile.

"Where have you been?" Tosh asked.

"Hiding. I followed those Hazak, as Bors calls them, having a feeling that you two would be close. I was right."

"What about the Gate?"

Tessa pointed upwards. Tosh saw the blue and pink sky of Ancient Mars. Then, the Gate appeared as if a camouflaged tarp was pulled off it.

"Shall we?"

The two nodded.

For three jumps, Tosh, Bors and Tessa travelled along. The Gate did its trick of cold air, chilling Tosh to the point he thought he'd freeze solid. After the fourth use of the Gate, Tessa held out her hand for the cube. Tosh handed it over without even thinking as they looked around. They were on a small hill that overlooked a town of huts and one long lonely spire. "I think I know where we are," Tosh whispered.

"Good, because according to the map, I have no idea where to go next," Tess a said.

"What do you mean?"

"Do you know what 'Nine Hammers of the Ram' means?" she asked, looking at him.

"None."

"You just said—"

Tosh held his hand up to stop Bors.

"*You* know where we are?" Tessa asked, givng Tosh a doubting look. "I barley know where we are now. Yet, you—"

"It's Mulkver. One of the last places in the Known Worlds that serves a decent kir."

"Can you point to it on the starmap?"

"No. Travelled here by a rocket, was rather drunk at the time." He stopped andturned towards the spire again. "However, I do know about a tavern here."

"Why does that not surprise me," Bors said with a groan.

"I'd be surprised if you didn't know one here," Tosh said, giving his friend...his *brother* a smile. "It's right up your alley. Brutal and violent. Or it can be."

"You mean *Tallinnn's*," Tessa said.

Both looked at her oddly, "How do you know of it?" They both asked, then gave each other a sidelong look.

"Only place to really drink around here. And I mean to get anything. The rest fo the planetoid, there is nothing."

The tavern *Tallinnn's* was much as Tosh remembered. It was the spire itself. A tall spire on the edge of town, with a much *much* larger space inside. Sets of steps led up to the higher levels, which Tosh said was where the more brutish unruly went to pass the time with brawling. Tessa looked around, amazed by the sights inside.

"You look like you've never been inside," Tosh said.

"I haven't."

Tosh stopped and looked at her. "Then, how did you know about this place?"

She shrugged. "Guessed?" She then blew him a kiss and traipsed off towards the stairs, pirouetting around a few people and humming to herself in the same strange tuneless music of hers.

There were more people than last time, yet that was to be expected. The smell was still the same, perfume and smoked meats hiding the sickly sweet smell of rot and puke. And when he ordered a kir and they didn't stare at him like he was a mutant near-human from Europa. He felt relief that it was still the same place.

"Dul Saan? Is that you?" A voice barked form the other side of the bar.

Tosh turned to see one of the men that ran *Tallinnn's*. Vas. "As I live and breathe, Vas?" Tosh shoved his hand out. He racked his brained trying to remember why he had used the name Dul Saan here.

"It is good to see you. You ever find that spice merchant?" Vas asked, giving Tosh a wink.

That's why. The little time he had tried to be a spicer had not ended well. It was another reason he had done it her eon the back of beyond. *Tallinnn's* was a bit of a backwater, even with Gates and rockets. Yet, it had sounded better than it was. He spent three weeks in the rooms here, without a way to get home. Then, Vas took pity and sent him home. Of course, Tosh had also to spend the last of the money he had conned out of Setter.

"They make your drink right?" Vas asked, pointing to the kir.

"They did. Thank you."

"You need anything, anything at all, give me a shout."

"Of course," Tosh said, giving Vas another hearty handshake. *Wonderful, he probably thinks he can pump more money out of me.*

Tosh looked over to see a man in a golden mask cavorting around, one that banished all thought of Vas. *That's odd.* Tosh watched the man over the rim of his glass of kir. He was glad he had found a bar that served the stuff properly. The only thing he really missed was absinthe. When he was done here, he would find one of the fables absinthe houses on Deneb Four. *If you find that damn Eye.*

The masked man moved again, catching Tosh's attention again. *Something about him…* The masked fellow moved around like someone who took in the entire place with wonder. The masked man was truly happy to be around people who were drinking and starting to whore before heading up to finish their business. Even Tosh thought about paying for a woman, Bors could have been three deep for all he knew. *Why not indulge myself while here?*

The masked man fixed dark globes that were the mask's eyes on Tosh. There was something about the look that disturbed Tosh. He continued to drink making eye contact with the masked fellow. After a handful of moments, the man made his way to Tosh. The robes the man wore were ostentatious. His own uncle Owen wore less flamboyant clothes, which was something since his uncle wore gold lamé and pink coats with ten-foot trains of silk and cloaks of jarring neon blue to cause people to be uncomfortable, but still accepted. *A flamboyant gay uncle is fine. But wanting to be a boy when born a girl is a step to far?*

He shook himself from the thought. "Hello," the golden masked man said, a smile in the masculine voice, his robes scintillated with colors as he spoke.

"Hello," Tosh said, taking in the speaker.

There were tiny gems stitched in that reflected some kind of internal light source which emerged from the robe itself, bathing the man and anyone within five feet in a riotous wave after wave of rainbow colors. The masked man shoved out a black silk gloved hand and said in a strange echoing voice, "Yes…sorry." The masked man shook his head a little. "Hello, we are Vostock of the Collective. What are you designated?"

"I am Tosh, formerly of the du'Vaul House," he said, not seeing the need to who he was out here. Then, bit his tongue since he wasn't sure if Vas heard or not.

"Why former?" Vostock asked, his masked head canted to one side like a dog that doesn't understand a command.

"I broke old laws and was kicked out," Tosh said. He wasn't sure why he said that. Or why he had said "formerly of the house." He looked over to see the bartender hadn't heard it and let out a breath.

Good, I can still drink a little more. Maybe get a girl, or a man. Or both.

Vostock moved closer, the golden mask leaning in very very close. Tosh could smell the scent of alcohol on Vostock's breath. "Why do you want a woman or a man? Or both? And, why does it matter if you are formerly of House du'Vaul or not, friend Tosh?" Vostock asked, moving even closer to Tosh. To a point Tosh was a little uncomfortable.

"Shh," Tosh said, placing a hand over the hole where the mask's "mouth" was. "I don't want to get kicked out."

"Is this guy bothering you, Dul Saan?" Vas asked Tosh, while staring at the masked Vostock.

For a moment, Tosh was about to say yes when he stopped and looked at the mask a little more closely. He saw something. An emblem that made him pull his hands away form the mask. "No Vas, I would like a private room for my friend and I. And, when I send for one, a woman and a man. Please."

"Of course," Vas said, giving Tosh a deep bow. "Anything for the House."

"Thank you," Tosh said.

Hurrying into a private suite, Tosh tugged at Bors' arm as they passed. The barbarian looked confused. When Bors turned his head towards Tosh, Tosh pointed towards the masked man. He shouted, "He is the key. He has an emblem of nine hammers around a ram."

"Why would the star map lead us to a person?" Tessa asked. She appeared from no where, yet Tosh didn't question it anymore.

"No idea," Tosh said. "But, he could be it."

Vostock was more that happy to have more people to talk to in the private suite, that he insisted to pay for himself. Said it was "research." The golden masked fellow plied them all with wine and drink. Tosh and Bors thought they could drink this man under the table, yet the masked man continued to speak, ask questions, laugh, and drink as Bors and Tosh's words grew more and more slur. Tessa was deep in her cups and was snoring softly on the table, Nix curled up in her jacket hood.

Tosh looked at the sleeping girl, shaking his head. *Such a youthful girl, can't hold her drink. But, at least she is a marvel.*

Vostock slammed down his tenth tumbler of bloodgin and let out a contented *sigh.* "I wish to take you to my home. Please, Friend Bors, Friend Tosh? Bring the youth?"

Bors glared at Vostock. "Why? Why bring the girl?"

"If not, the temporal wave will make us lose her."

"What?"

Vostock pulled out a thick disk. "If she doesn't come, she will worry. She won't know where we are, and we can't have that. Do not worry, I have a portable transmatt device here that will fit all of us. Coming?" He asked as he pushed a button on the thick disk without waiting for a reply.

Before any of them could say anything, there was a flash of light and they were in a different place. Tosh felt a shift and felt himself dragged to the floor.

"Where are we?" He aske,d looking around.

"Why, my home," Vostock said with a laugh. "The Home of the Nine Hammers of the Ram."

CHAPTER ELEVEN

Tosh was shocked by the sheer luxury of the palace the three found themselves in. Sumptuous offerings were pale descriptors of the place. The walls were made of gold, murals of strange animals and unknown alien planet vistas adorned the walls, ceiling and frescoes on the floor. Some made with gems that were used as common art supplies. The food offered was more than he had been given when he was a youth in House du'Vaul, and even when he was with his father for a dinner party to one of the Twelve Families, the fair provided by Vostock and the rest of his Collective made the food from the Twelve Families taste like sterile air and food paste.

Upon arrival, Vostock was met by another masked and similarity adored form. "Please, you must meet the others. This is Burble," Vostock said, indicating the one that met them at the cavernous door to the complex. This one with a silver mask and green orbs for eyes.

"You are a strange one," the masked Burble said, the dark eyes of the mask falling first on Tosh. Moving forward with a mincing step, the form closed in on Tosh. When the figure was closer, Tosh detected perfume in the air. Things that his family traded before he left. A scent tickled Tosh's brain, an image of his mother kissing him on the cheek.

"You are such a beautiful young one, my little jewel." His mother had said.

"Are you well?" Burble asked, leaning closer.

Tosh shook his head and looked at the mask. Since it was closer, he saw the silver was real, not some plated metal. Burble also had six fingers on each hand, two thumbs that looked strange and alien, one on either side of the hand.

"What delineation are you?" Tosh asked.

"Why, my child, we are not descended from some common stock of near-humans. We are a pure strain. The *true* form of Man!" Burble said with a laugh.

Tosh looked at the thumbs and shook his head. "I think otherwise."

Bors gave out a cough. Tosh looked over to see the large man was shaking his head. He mouthed, "To many."

Tosh shook his head at the barbarian. He turned back to the masked person. "You can't be pure human."

"But we are. We have transcended," the masked form said, the last few words a singsongy praise. The form made a gesture like a gesticulation to the roof.

Tosh turned his eyes upwards and saw more of the mural that had started in the antechamber. Before he could get a closer look, the form reached out to grab onto Tosh's right arm. "You, you could be one of us as well."

"How so?" Tosh asked.

The masked man chuckled. "Many ways." A wicked grin mixed with the words made Tosh uneasy.

"Please, you must be tired from the journey. Shall we eat and rest?" Vostock asked, pulling Tosh closer to him, leading the three deeper into the complex.

"What do you do here?" Tessa asked. She looked a little nervous and Nix was curled tight around her shoulder. The head snapping this way and that, tasting the air and giving disapproving hisses.

"We mostly think and ponder the ways of the universe," Burble said from Tessa's right. Tosh saw that the girl shied away from Burble, even from Vostock. She kept close to Bors and the barbarian extended an arm and hand for the youth to take, which she did with a thankful look.

"Yet, we met you—"

"Out and about, yes," Vostock said, spinning around and clapping his hands. "I am the Seeker for the next few hundred years. I go out and seek those who might need help, or who seem interesting. Or will be fun company," he said.

"So, we are here because we are good company?" Bors asked.

Burble turned the silver mark towards Vostock. "Well, yes, *someone* will think you are *fascinating* company."

"Come, you should speak to the head of our order."

"Who?" Tosh asked.

Vostock turned mum, which Tosh thought was strange. He then watched as the hallways branched out again and again, some ending in staircases, other to what he thought were lifts. One, he turned to see a group much like their own motely crew walking around a corner. He stopped and was about to ask what that was when Burble muttered, "Time dialation, happens here sometimes."

Tosh looked at her. "What?"

"We don't have time," Burble said. "The ceremony will start soon. The Head of the Order wishes to speak to you all before that." She then looked at Tosh and Tosh felt exposed and laid bare before those jade colored orbs. He to moved a little closer to Bors.

The sound that started to rattle then thunder through the rich hallways picked up the deeper they went. Tosh felt something was *wrong* with the sounds. He saw that Tessa and Bors felt the same way.

"Tell us again, why did you choose us, Vostock?"

Vostock more animated than he was since he had arrived in the House of Nine Hammers of the Ram turned and grabbed Tosh by the arms. There was real strength in the hands. "I'm sent out to find people in need help."

"Desperation?" Tessa said.

"Something like that, child of the Gate," Vostock said.

"How did you—"

Before she could respond, Burble cut in, "Quiet child." She touched

Tessa on the head and she stopped talking, her eyes growing glassy and she walked more like an automaton than a person.

Bors roared and tried to swing at Burble, yet Vostock was at the large man's side in the blink of an eye. He grabbed a hold of Bors arm and whispered something that Tosh thought sounded like, "Quiet." The large barbarian started to move along much like Tessa.

Vostock and Burble turned their masked faces to Tosh. "I will go and wont say anything," Tosh said, holding his hands up. "No need for that."

"Good," they both said at once and Tosh followed, feeling dread roil his stomach.

"That's a good ape," Burble said.

Tosh was silent and didn't take the jib.

———

Following the pair of masked beings, Tosh found himself in a large domed chamber with a half dozen other masked forms. They all were about Vostock's middling height, a few a little plumper and one or two skinny robed folk. All had masks of different metals. The one Vostock went to had a mask of something akin to silver, but there was a different luster to it.

"Leader, I present—"

The leader held up a hand, cutting off Vostock. "You three come at a wondrous time. We were about to start the ritual. Questions are for after."

Tosh was silent as the group of masked forms moved around an oblong table he hadn't seen when he first entered the domed chamber. In the center was the woman, who could have been a copy of the woman from The Drumgag's lair. She was chained by golden shackles at her wrists and ankles in the center stretched out spread eagle, and still as stone.

"Why is she—"

"Relax, it is for your own good," Burble said. "She is a liar and a thief."

Tosh didn't know what to do. Bors and Tessa still looked classy eyed and he didn't think he get out without their help. So, he stayed and watched and waited.

The leader in the platinum mask threw up his hands, the others did the same. Soon there was a glow coming from the assembled group, not from their clothing but from their outstretched hands. And, it came from the woman herself. The glow was joined by a low guttural chant that came from Vostock and the others. It grew louder and louder in the oddly echoing that issued form the mouths of those around the table. A blue light started to come from the woman. She started moving, then her body went as stiff as a board. She rose from the table, her wrists and ankle cuffs straining to hold her from floating away. A rictus of pain on her face.

The glow rose from her and as the chanting grew louder and louder, buzzing in Tosh's heard more and more intense. Tosh felt as though his skull had filled with wasps. It grew to a crescendo and then all the sound left the room.

The glow, first as a trickle, then faster and faster, left the woman and entered the gathered people, though not Tosh, Bors or Tessa. As the light left, the woman dropped to the table, boneless. She gasped and cried, weakly mewling and coughing. "Please," she gasped, turning to the masked forms. "Please release me. You can't treat the Eye of Saturnalia this way."

Tosh was stunned. *A woman? We were sent to find a woman?*

Bors at that moment shook his head. "We have to do something, brother," Bors said.

"What? They can easily destroy us," Tosh said.

"Very true," Vostock said. He gestured with his hand and large white ape creatures appeared from the shadows, grabbing Tosh, Bors and Tessa with ease. "Now, we will have to put you away for a time. Until you choose to join the Collective, or die."

CHAPTER TWELVE

"You know Bors, I'm starting to get the feeling that you are a bad luck charm."

"Why would you say that, brother?"

"Half the places you take me to, we are captured at some point."

"We have to escape," Bors said.

"Yes, but how?" Tosh asked. "Can you summon your Gate yet?" He asked looking at Tessa.

Tessa shook her head. "No. They are blocking it somehow. Which, if it were so vile and painful, would be a really *Friday* thing to witness."

Tosh didn't even attempt to ask her what she meant. He instead looked to Bors. "I doubt we will be able to escape the same—"

The door opened as he spoke and one of the masked people of the Collective appeared. The body then slumped forward into the cell and the near nude for of the woman that the three had seen chained to a table strode in, looking at each of them in turn. "Hello, this is your time to escape."

Bors didn't say anything, he started forward into hallway. Tosh looked at the woman. "How did you—"

"Don't be *Tuesday,* Tosh. We need to go," Tessa said, sliding by him to join Bors in the hallway.

"Coming?" the woman asked, looking from him to the hallway and back.

Tosh looked at her. He didn't trust her at all. *Something is very weird and wrong here.* He took a step forward and reached to touch the woman. She recoiled.

"We don't have time for play," the woman said, looking at Tosh.

Tosh shook his head as she strode out of the chamber. *Something is very wrong here.* He felt a strange disconnect, when he looked at the hallway, Bors and Tessa were gone. He blinked and moved towards the hallway and saw the three of them down the end of a long hallway, waving him forward.

"But, how—"

"Come on, brother," Bors said.

Tosh staggered forward, feeling lightheaded. He staggered against the wall and felt drained, as if moving another step would be to taxing. He saw Bors and Tessa leaving him behind. The eyes of the woman stared at him for a moment before she too disappeared.

He dropped his head into his hands, feeling weak and powerless. "What is going on?"

"Brother," are you well?"

Tosh looked up and saw that he was still in the cell with Bors and Tessa, Bors standing over him. "What is—"

"You walked towards the door and slammed your head against it. I had to stop you. You then dropped to the ground."

Tosh reached up to feel his head hurt, blood starting to run down his face. "What is going on?"

"I don't know," Tessa said. "But, Nix is concerned." The serpent hissed, looking around, constantly moving at the slightest noise, his tongue flicking out, tasting the air.

"The last thing I saw was the woman appearing and taking you two out ahead to escape, leaving me," Tosh said as Bors pressed a cloth to Tosh's forehead.

"That didn't happen," Bors said. "You pounded your head—"

"I heard you the first time, Bors. And I can feel the pain in my head."

Tosh looked at the cloth, wondering where Bors had gotten it. It was a gaudy piece of golden cloth. It was cool to the touch and it did feel good against the pain at his scalp. He then heard a titter of laughter and looked to one shadowed area of the cell. He thought he caught the sight of a gaudy robe like his captors wore.

"Tosh, what is wrong?"

Tosh looked at Bors. "Nothing. I thought I saw something in the shadows."

"Always jumping at shadows, aren't you," Bors with a grin.

Tosh turned to face Bors. "Its how you appeared. So maybe—"

"Nonsense."

Tosh quirked an eyebrow. "Bors. Where did we meet?" Tosh asked. He also closed his mind off, it wasn't much. But there was something in the back of his head.

"We met…we met…in a cell. I bested you at a contest. You came to free me," Bors said, giving Tosh a laugh.

"Why do you call me brother? What were we fighting?" Tosh asked, pushing himself to his feet and backing away a step. He then thought of the bandits he faced before coming to find Bors.

Bors let out a laugh. "Come now. We were fighting the bandits together. They captured us and—"

Tosh smirked and jerked his head towards the shadowy corner. "Nice try."

Bors stopped at that moment, everything did. The form of Bors melted away, as did Tessa, Nix and the stone cell. Instead, he was seated on a plush chair, looking at one of the Collective.

"Well, I thought I could bluff my way through," the copper masked woman said. "Worth a shot."

Tosh glared at the woman in the mask. There was a rage he felt, something he thought he had only felt for his father. "You tried to tinker with my mind. For *fun?*"

The copper masked woman gave him a shrug. "It is a boring—"

Before she could finish, Tosh struck out with his hand, hitting her in the chest. She gasped, doubling over. Tumbling from her chair, she tried to reach for something on her belt. "You...you horrible—" .

Tosh kicked her hard to make her stop. He kicked the small raygun she was reaching for from her grasp. "I might be, yet I don't tinker in people's heads for fun." Tosh stepped over the crying woman, scooped up the raygun and left the room. He turned and burned the door closed with the lances of crimson from the raygun.

The hallway was a riot of gold and silver arches with a marble stone floor, polished to a bright sheen and a runner of dark green and black along the center. He had no idea where to go, he listened and couldn't hear anything. There were a few other doors that he hesitated to try nearby, yet each one was empty. Each also had a stink of someone who'd been there a very long time.

He continued down the corridor, the décor changing as he did. It grew more utilitarian, less polished metal. The floor grew rougher and less polished. Until at last after hundred of yards, he was in a rough hewn stone tunnel. The light from the floating sconces was gone. He had taken one of the last drifting globes and tethered it to himself, following the large tunnel. There were a few branching tunnels that he didn't go down, the reek of animals drifted towards him from the dark side branches.

At last, he came to the end of the tunnel. There was a large black iron gate of a jail cell. Inside, he saw the same woman from earlier. She was tied to the wall, without a stitch of clothing. It didn't feel right. Part of him expected to appear in another chamber with a masked Collective member. Yet, he had to see if she was real or not. *She looked so real.*

"Who are you?" the woman asked, looking up.

"I've come to rescue you," Tosh said. "Well, my friends and I have."

"How?"

He didn't have a key, yet he did have the pistol. He burned the door lock open, pulled it open and felt winded. She gave him an awkward glance as he huffed for a moment. "You are here to resuce me?"

"We were sent to find the Eye of Saturnalia. And that is you, right?"

"One of my names, but I prefer Ella," the woman said. "Who sent you?"

"He calls himself *The Master*, but—"

At that moment, there was a roar coming from the tunnel.

"We need to get out of here," she said. "Please, untie me."

Tosh was looking at that and realized he could not untie her. The ropes and knots looked complex and almost Gordian. "I don't think I..." He stopped, looked at the raygun in the sash of his robe. *Worked for Alexander.*

Tosh withdrew the small ray pistol. He wasn't good at it, since the training was for boys and not girls. He shook his head and took as careful a bead as he could and fired. The brilliant ruby lance of light struck the ropes holding the girl without burning her. Tosh smiled. *Might be able to seal that deal after this.* He turned as another roar echoed down the hall. "We might have an issue."

Tosh turned to see a giant four-armed ape-like creature barrelling towards him. He spun, firing the ray gun at the creature. He fired again and again. Yet, his hands kept shaking and the rays kept hissing by the ape thing, singing the fur and hair. Tosh never scoring a hit. Behind the ape create, Tosh thought he saw Bors charging down the corridor after the beast. *Will he get here in time?* Twice, the ruby lances skittered close to the large barbarian.

Tosh and the woman rushed to the door to try and swing it shut. At the last second, they closed it. The creature grabbed the door and with a might scream of beastial fury, it tore the door from its hinges.

The creature roared as it neared Tosh, it reared up and swung down with its four arms. Bors travelled past the creature and slammed into the smaller man, tackling him, driving them both away from the reach of the creature. Bors looked at Tosh and nodded. Tosh shakily nodded. "Thank you."

"Of course, brother." Bors then turned and slammed his sword into the creature, taking one of its arms. It let out a squeal and slammed Bors aside. The three hands went for Ella and Tosh.

Tosh raised the raygun and fired again and again. There was a squeal and the smell of brunt fur. Toshed opened his eyes and was shocked to see he had killed the thing.

"How are we going to get out of here?" Bors said, as he pushed himself up. Tosh was at his side, helping the large man up.

"No idea." Tosh then shook his head.

The woman smiled. "Please. I can help."

"How?" Bors asked.

Ella's fingers snapped and the five of them were outside of *Tallinnn's*. Tessa looked dazed and Nix shot into Tessa's sleeve.

"How did you—"

Tosh stopped Tessa with a slash of his hand. "Talk later, we need to leave. Now!"

"Where do you need to go?" Ella asked. "I can—"

"You could have done that at any time?" Bors asked.

"Yes, and no," Ella said. "Suffice to say that when Tosh freed me, I had full access to my powers."

Tosh looked at her. "The Drumgag."

CHAPTER THIRTEEN

There was a flash of something familiar to Tosh, an indigo flash. And the five of them were back before the façade of The Drumgag. Ella was wearing a modest dress. Tosh wanted to ask how all of this happened, yet he chalked it up to *The Master* playing around more. *Or the power of the Eye.*

Without missing a beat, Tessa stepped up to Tosh. "I still require my payment," Tessa said, her hand held out for the cube.

Tosh dropped it into her hands. "By all means, a deal is a deal." He then looked at Ella. "How are we going to—"

"What? You are going to give me to that loathsome thing?"

"The Drumgag is going to want a jewel. And we are not going to hand Ella over to them," Bors said.

"I am sure he will take that bauble you have, Master Tosh," Ella said, her eyes looking at the small satchel at Tosh's side.

Tosh pulled out a red and blue scintillating orb the size of an apple. After studying it for a moment, he nodded. "I am sure The Drumgag will take it. Since no one knows what the Eye of—"

"Please stop using that title," Ella said. "I hate it."

"Very well."

· · ·

The Drumgag looked at the jewel in Tosh's hands. "Give!" He screamed, thrusting his pathetic small flabby arm outward to get the gem from Tosh. The redhead at his side reached out to take it and The Drumgag yanked on the chain, pulling the woman back against his corpulent body. "Mine, you *sow!*"

Tosh tossed him the gem. He didn't watch as The Drumgag fought with his woman to grab the thing. He and Bors made for the exit with haste.

The Master shifted them once they started leaving The Drumgag's chamber. The tall lanky form appeared to be eager. Ella looked mildly annoyed at the man. "I am so glad you have—"

Before he could finish, Ella stomped towards him, the glow coming off of her growing brighter and brighter and shredding her clothes. Tosh watched in shock as the lanky tall form of *The Master* grew smaller and smaller until he was standing shoulder to shoulder with the near nude Ella. She reached out and slapped him hard across the masked face.

The strike tore the mask from the silken shroud to reveal a chubby man, a small set of green tinted pince nez glasses set askew by her strike His eyes were a very human brown that looked at Ella like a puppy whose master had kicked it for pissing on the carpet. He looked at her, bewildered.

"Husband! Why did you send these two for me? I was not done with my research."

"You were taking *soooooooo* long. A millennia has passed. I missed you," he said reaching out to touch her.

She pulled away. "You stupid pile of—"

She reached back to slap him again when he cowered and she glared at him a moment. Her visage went from hard and stony to softer and softer. "I will have to say, I did miss you as well."

"Really?"

"For a decade of two."

"Lovie..." The Master said in a lovesick tone. It made the bile rise in Tosh's throat.

Then, Ella said, "Darling."

The two embraced.

Bors and Tosh looked at each other, dumbstruck. "What are—"

"Wife?" The pair both asked.

"Oh yes. Thank you for your help. You two may leave," Ella said.

Before either could say anything, Ella gestured and the two found themselves in a wineshoppe. Tosh guessed somewhere on Mars judging by the shift in gravity and sudden dusty air.

"What just happened?" Bors asked, looking at Tosh with eyes bulging.

"I think we brought back a somewhat abusive wife to her co-dependent husband."

Bors shrugged "They have great power. I don't wish to get between those two."

"Me either. But, I think we both got what we wanted."

"How so?" Bors asked.

The two ordered food and drink, Tosh and Bors found their purses filled with coin that weren't there a moment before. "Well, for one, we have full purses and empty bellies. I say we change one of those."

As the meal came to them, Bors asked again, "How did we both get what we—"

"You have your sword still."

Bors touched the baldric and nodded. "Yes, but you—"

"You consider me to be a brother of your tribe?"

"Yes," Bors said, taking a long pull of his ale. "How else would I see you?"

"Then, my boon has been given. I have coin to continue with the procedure. And, I have a friend. Let's get another round."

In the back of Tosh's mind, he knew that the words were enough. Ella and *The Grifter* were together. He would drink to being free from them. He would be able to find another way to get what he wanted.

"What about Tessa?"

"I am sure the Guildie will be fine. She is tougher than she looks," Tosh said with a smile.

Bors smiled at that. The two clanked their tankards together and drank until the morning.

LAST PAGE

SPACE RANGER: MARS

PART OF THE KNOWN WORLD SERIES

LON VARNADORE

SPACE RANGER: MARS

PART ONE

R ick Tavish stepped off the last rung of his personal Space
Ranger rocket ship. The puff of red-orange dust settled to the
ground as he took his first step onto the planet. Some of it stained the
off-white boots. His eyes sought the bent landing strut from his landing. *Knew that landing felt wrong.* He shrugged, *any landing you can
walk away from.* The bent landing strut would be a mark on his record
of his first solo patrol. He was away from the main Space Ranger
Station surrounding Luna. Rick felt excitement buzz in his chest like
bees. He was ready to go on his first solo patrol. *Go by the numbers,
stick to the schedule, and the rest of the solo patrol will succeed.*

The Plains of Mars were cold and barren. Rick scanned the horizon
with his suit's instruments, which gave him data of the surrounding
area. The air was thin, but breathable. With the dust settling from his
landing, none of the rust-tinged dust would affect his breathing, his
suit's movements, or diagnostics. He would have to test himself every
night to make sure, but he was only on the planet for a few days before
he was onto the next leg of his patrol. The bubble helmet lit up with a
soft green fluorescence to assure him that the air was breathable before
he removed his helmet. *By the numbers.* It was still a regulation that he

wanted to respect, like not tearing his helmet off like he did in training. And he was given demerits for it. He touched the sides of his helmet and hit the catches. There was a hiss of pneumatic air, and the dry, thin air of Mars struck him hard. His mouth and nose felt the sudden dryness, and the sinus pain was enough for a quick headache that made him blink back tears.

It was strange, breathing air on another planet. A range of smells that were foreign struck him. The rust-tinged air was something that his brain would filter out soon. The incredibly dry air already robbed his throat of moisture, causing him to grab the canteen and squirt a dose of water into his mouth. He turned his mind towards getting his patrol under way.

Turning to his ship again, he smiled. *Let's get this started.* He hit a button on his left gauntlet. A side hatch in the rocket's sleek silver exterior split open. A large multi-hinged robotic limb lowered his large silver—and—red gear pod to the red soil.

The gear pod opened when it touched down, unsealing itself like a gift that unwrapped for Rick. It was a standard- issue pod, one that any Space Ranger with basic training could use to survive the in the climes and environs of the Known Worlds that the Space Rangers patrolled and protected. Several small shelves split open and slid out and up, creating a multi-levelled shelf for him to choose from. It reminded him of his grandfather's ancient carpenter's toolbox that he carried whenever he went to make a repair. When asked why he took the whole thing for a simple job, his grandfather said, "Never know what tool you might need."

Rick's eyes skipped over several rows, since those held items or replacements needed for planets like Venus or the Jovian and Saturnine moons for air units and rebreathers. He would need those for the later legs of his patrol, but for now, he could ignore them. His eyes then went to the food rations and the water converter and purifier. He took up the purifier, an oval attachment that clipped to the back of his suit and attached to his belt. Then, he heard the internal clicking of his suit. It would help draw excess moisture from the air and anything that he expelled to help fill the small emergency canteen, even recycle any other moisture expelled from his body. Once it had been an all-in-one system, but when the modular design had been found to work better, the Rangers took to keeping the compartments separate until truly needed. Then he slipped food ration packets into their compartments at his lower back. Finally, he took up his Tellic ray pistol, a sleek pistol with a blunted muzzle and a DNA scanner in the grip. It connected to his space suit gauntlet, which had an override to the scanner. Yet he still needed to activate it or the ray pistol wouldn't work at all.

He initiated the sequence for the Tellic, felt the suit's right palm buzz with a slight electrical field as the DNA scanner readied itself to scan the weapon. He detached the Tellic from his gauntlet and took up the grip. There was a green dot that appeared on the butt end of the Tellic. *Ready to use, if I have a need to.* He slipped the ray gun into the holster hanging a few inches below his right hip. It was a quick-draw designed holster, though the Space Rangers weren't to draw without need. *Without a great need,* his instructors had drilled into him, deep, deep into his head.

But, he was on a planet torn apart by civil strife. It was one of the reasons he had chosen Mars to start his solo patrol on this planet. It would need the help of a Ranger. The nearest city was Gods' Rest, over a thousand miles from where he was. It was nestled in the shadow of Olympus Mons. And it would be one of the last stops of his patrol. The human cities of Gods' Rest, Janden Gap, and Pyrrc needed the help from the Space Rangers once and again to help with the Green Martians and Golgoro kingdoms. He was here to mediate and to protect. The patrols were mandatory, and Rick felt proud to be on Mars. It had been his dream to come to the red planet for so long, and he was finally here. The way the missions were set up, the Ranger's Central Command weighed every decision and every need versus what a Ranger was capable of. Even with that in mind, Rick wasn't positive he was the right one, deep down. He still felt too green, though his enthusiasm and courage pushed those doubts aside when he was first given the mission.

No, I am ready. Command wouldn't have given me this patrol if they thought I wasn't ready.

Standing alone on the planet's surface, knowing that the only one to rely on was himself, was when the true gravity of his position hit him. *I am alone on this planet.* There *were* contacts in the human cities, true. Even in the two kingdoms, there were contacts that Rick could tap if he had to. However, he had to rely on himself while on the planet.

The communicator blinked on his right gauntlet. He tapped the icon, and it created a bust holo with the striking features of the face of Tsan Xi, the head of Ranger Command. "Everything going according to regulations, Ranger Tavish?"

"Yes ma'am," he said, giving her a salute. "I have the gear pod unloaded. Was about to break out the rocket sledge."

"And the rocket pack backup?" She asked, arching a thin eyebrow.

"Yes ma'am, was about to attach that now." He felt himself blush for having to be reminded.

Without missing a beat, Xi said, "Rangers lead the way."

"Rangers lead the way," Rick said as the holo disappeared.

With the help from the rocket's other loading arm, he settled the rocket sledge to the sand, the phrase which he and Commander Xi said to each other rang in his head. He knew that the origins of the Rangers, or at least where the phrase came from was during the dark days of World War Two and the landing on Normandy. A unit of army rangers had lost their captain during the first onslaught of landing under fire. A general, Norman Cota, found them, told him who they were, and he said, "Rangers lead the way," and the phrase became the Rangers motto.

After the war, and after the eventual forced peace with the Communists of the U.S.S.R. against the common threat of the invasion of squidheads from Europa, Earth was united in a single vision within ten years of the end of World War Two. All focused on one thing, to reach for the stars. And the Rangers led the way. And, today, a hundred years after the landing of Normandy—almost to the day—they still lead the way to the stars beyond Pluto to the other Known Worlds. His patrol was one small part of a larger destiny of the Rangers and the Coalition in general.

He took a step towards the sledge and had forgotten about gravity for a second. His movement launched him forward a good foot more than he wanted, barking his shin against the sledge. His suit absorbed the impact. The embarrassment still stung. *Why are you being so green, ranger?* Shaking his head he muttered to himself, "Head in the game, Rick."

Turning to focus on the sledge, he attached the rocket pack rig to the harness, and settled onto the sledge. He took a quick sip of the water from his canteen, took a deep draught of the dry and dusty air, and replaced the helmet. Once it locked on, he tapped a series of codes into his left gauntlet, and the ship locked itself up tight. Even the gear pod wrapped itself back up and waited for him to return from his patrol.

Try to remember where you parked, he thought to himself with a smirk. He laughed at the small joke and settled onto the sledge. He twisted the throttle of the rocket sledge and shot off towards the first place on his patrol.

He would begin in the ancient and dead city of Lotus. The land sped by him in a long, continuous plane of red-orange sand and rocks. The large white pillars of the outer gates of Lotus loomed into view as Rick's sledge shot around the foothills of the City of Lotus proper. As he drew closer, the red-orange sandstone gateways appeared. They were carved from the nearby hills, but no one in the Science Corp knew where the white polished stone for the city proper had come from. The large gateways had an Oriental flare to them, but that was impossible since, according to the Science Corp, the city had been dead tens of thousands of years ago.

The archways formed a winding pathway that some in the Corp said was the main roadway, and they had found pieces of the gates as far as Dalcan, the capital of Thrane, the Green Martian leader. He didn't look forward to meeting that particular individual. Still, he expected that the saurian creature would try and get his suit; this had been his constant plan for any ranger that came to the city or even into the Green Martian lands.

The City of Lotus was immense. A gargantuan city, carved from a white sandstone-like material, which was an unknown stone on Mars. One of the rumors he had heard from his friends in Science Corp was that the blocks were from Earth, and the Empire of Lotus, as it was colloquially named, ruled all the planets in the solar system at one time. Yet, beyond this one city, nothing else remained of those who ruled it or the remnants of an empire on any other planet. The frescoes and bas-reliefs were humanoid, and it led some in the Corp to think Mankind was a descendant of them. This sounded strange and wrong to Rick. Science had established that Man had started on Earth.

Once he reached the wide gates of Lotus, he entered the opening between the gateposts, which was wide enough to play football—the American version—between them. The walls were fifty feet high and contained a tomb rather than a dead city. Any bodies had long ago dried up and returned to dust. Rick doubted he would find anything, but he had to go through the city in a grid pattern that covered a fifth of the entire city to search for anything. Part of the patrol. In case some Ranger might catch something that hadn't been seen by aerial photos, satellites, or the thirty other patrols that were sent through the City of Lotus before Rick.

His gauntlet blinked when he reached the city. He said, "Map, City of Lotus grid," and a HUD sprang up inside his helmet. It revealed a path to navigate around his section of the city to explore. The last three Space Rangers had done their job, and he was going to do his own scouting.

Entering the city, he took a sharp right and started down a long, broad, stone-paved street, his sledge hovering a few inches off the ground and not causing any harm to the actual stone. Though, from what he had seen and heard from Science Corp, nothing short of an atomic could even cause a scratch in the white stone. He hit a four-way street rather suddenly, and his map angled him off to his right. His eyes slid to the left, and for a second, he thought he saw a shadow. He snapped his head to the left, and whatever it was was gone. For a handful of moments, he waited, taking long, steady breaths from his suit. The air supply was at ninety percent. He *could* breathe the Martian atmosphere a little if he needed, yet he wanted to keep his helmet on if he could help it. It wouldn't be great, but he could save the suit some wear and tear if he needed to take off the helm. The suit was his key to everything back on the ship. And it was his to guard.

The suit was the reason the Green Martians wanted him. Especially their leader, Thrane, who wanted a Space Ranger suit so badly. With it, the saurian Martian thought he could gain control of a Ranger's ship. Then the cowardly creature would use it to try and attack Ranger Command. One of the Thranes, two decades ago, had tried it and nearly succeeded. Had it not been for the help of a Golgoro psi-blade, Command would have been attacked by a small Trojan Horse ship. It was the reason suits were now DNA-locked to one person only.

Granted, there were plans that had been put into place since. It was still something that Rick didn't want to have befall him and his suit. Even the Golgoro wanted the suit to find out how the helmet shielded the Rangers from their mind-control powers.

He turned his head to the right again, seeing the blinking path illuminated before him. Again, he turned his head left and felt something, *someone* calling him. *Don't do it. Stay the course.* But that little niggling doubt continued to chip away, and Rick started to turn the control yoke to the right.

He turned the sledge to the left and twisted the throttle a half rotation. It started to slew to the left, and his helmet flickered with a warning. PATH DEVIATION, WARNING PATH DEVIATION. Rick grumbled in his throat. Another demerit. Yet, *it could be something.* He let out a sigh and said, "Override, Space Ranger Rick Tavish, authorization number 5498204."

The suit went quiet. It still illuminated his path behind him with an angry red glow coming from behind him. He turned to see the map, and his path was still laid out for him in the suit's HUD. As he moved the sledge down the long, corridor-like passage, a sense of dread filled him. "Maybe this wasn't such a good idea." He looked up, and there were spans of bridges thirty feet up that crisscrossed in random patterns that made him blink his eyes before looking back ahead of him.

He had to slow the sledge to a near-crawl to make the tight turn ahead when something slammed into his sledge. The force of the impact crashed hard into him, and the sledge slammed into the wall. His right leg was pinned against the pure white wall. He let out a grunt of pain. The suit registered the pain and injected a small pain reliever in his arm.

Something grabbed at his helmet hard, trying to wrench it free from behind. His right hand grabbed his ray pistol and jerked it out. He fired when he saw the pale, skinny thing that had slammed into him, grabbing at the helmet again. It squalled in pain and dropped to the ground, part of its right shoulder atomized by the Tellic ray pistol. It looked much like a chimpanzee, except it was covered in coarse white fur, and its eyes were red with slitted green pupils. The hands were much like a human hand, while the feet were more simian-like, with a long tail that he thought could aide in balance.

Rick looked over the thing to see it was not alone. There was a tribe of thirty of these monkey-sized pale creatures. They had somehow gotten a stone loose and used it to pin the sledge against the wall. They held crude spears of rust-tinged metal that they thrust towards Rick, not getting close enough to actually strike him. Yet, all of them cowered before the ray pistol that Rick held. One of them crept forward and started to jabber in its language at Rick. Its hands were held up, showing they were empty. Rick swung his Tellic in a wide arc, not firing, but still not trusting these creatures fully.

The creature that was talking to him babbled and it sounded like something like "Baa ba baab babba," before the Ranger translator unit kicked in. It needed a few moments to find the right language to help make it work. Many linguists had worked to program the translator with hundreds of languages, yet not all of them worked. The words were translated into, "We need your kill gun. Do not shoot us. Shoot the ones who control us. Please. Need help."

Rick followed the bony finger of the monkey-thing towards the center of the city. There, he saw a tower that looked plain and unadorned as usual. Then, he continued to look and saw small pennants and banners on it that wouldn't have been seen from fellow Space Rangers unless they had directly looked at it. Something didn't make sense. *Those banners shouldn't be there.*

"We need your help," the creature said again.

"Then, why did he attack me," Rick asked, pointing at the dead monkey-thing.

"He wasn't supposed to. I think that...he...was...kill...kill! *Kill!*"

The leader of the monkey-things lunged for Rick, fury and rage looked to boil through the group of creatures that all started to chatter the same thing that the translator screamed in his ears as "*Kill! Kill! Kill!*" He fired his ray pistol, cutting the leader in half. The other monkey-things started screeching and hooting as the leader died. They jumped up and down, throwing down their spears, surging forward with only their hands out. Rick could see small glinting claws sliding out of their fingers like a cat's claw.

Rick grabbed the throttle and twisted hard, The sledge shot forward, plowing into several of the insane monkey-creatures. He took a glance in the side mirrors and saw them running towards him, some hurling spears awkwardly, as if they didn't know how to throw them. Most were climbing the buildings and running on four legs along the second story bridges coming towards him. Rick turned his head forward. Had he not, he would have missed the barrier raising up before him. He yanked his steering handles hard to the right, and the sledge skidded into the barrier before streaking past the wailing creatures that had shown up in droves. The barrier that he sideswiped was made of a dark stone, what could have been crates made of wood from who-knows-where, and even discarded Ranger cargo pods. Still, Rick hadn't slammed headlong into the barrier and was able to shoot away from the trap and the creatures.

Rick looked at the gauge, thankful the fuel was nuclear fusion and wasn't in need of refueling. Though the banging around was not too worrisome, the sledge wasn't designed to take that kind of abuse for long. He then saw a large, open square coming up and saw something he didn't think he'd see for another week.

A throne with a Golgoro woman was in the middle of the square. She was smiling as she lounged in the intricate throne of metal. She was nearly naked, except for a few gauzy clothes that revealed more than hid her form. She was a pale, red-skinned woman with milky white hair. The square thronged with more monkey-creatures, chittering and hooting as the sledge came into the square. He stopped it, turning behind him to see the creatures closing the gap and moving closer.

He pulled out his pistol, aiming it at the woman. "Stop it. Turn off your mind-control beams, or I'll shoot," he shouted.

"The Golgoro mind-control beams aren't affecting them. They worship me as their Goddess, without the need for beams. She smiled as she spoke, a lustful look on her face. Rick was glad that the helmet's audio filters helped to stop the vocal trickery that could seduce someone not prepared.

"How is that—"

Rick didn't get any further. Something slammed into his back. He was punched and kicked and stomped on by many of the monkey-creatures. They screeched and hooted, and Rick eventually had his head struck against the side of his helmet one too many times. His head ringing, he dropped to the ground before the creatures swarmed him.

————

Rick Tavish found himself face-to-face with the pale, red-skinned woman from Golgoro. He was strapped down, the suit still on him, and the helmet protected his mind from any possible rays of mind control, since the little creatures couldn't find a way to tug off the helm. It was covered in a thin film of body oils and some musk that permeated the seams of his suit.

"What is the meaning of this?" Rick shouted, finding himself tied to the throne, kneeling. He had to look up at the pale woman. He was still in a fog from the concussion. His suit's HUD was trying to mend him as best it could. "I'm a Space Ranger, what—"

"Beloved, so good for you to come to see me."

"What?" He asked, shaking his head as he came out of the fog. The HUD stated he had a concussion and he realized he would need to stay conscious. He then felt a small bite in his arm and felt a rush of vitamins and a serum to wake him up. *Well, at least the suit still works.* "What are you talking about? How can I be your beloved?"

She moved closer, her hips moved in a seductive swaying that caused Rick's heart to race, even without the stims from the suit. She gave him a broad white smile. "I have seen it. You and I will be wed one day. And I came to the city you call Lotus to wait for you." A pale hand stretched out to touch his shoulder while she leaned down to expose more and more of her curvaceous form under the loose wrapping of gauzy fabric that clung to her skin.

"And these creatures?" Rick asked, indicating the monkey-creatures that moved about. Around forty of them chittered away, some swinging and moving. All of them had their big, round eyes focused on the pale, red-skinned woman.

"A woman has her hobbies," she said with a cold and sadistic smile. "You don't approve?" She asked when she saw the frown on Rick's face.

"Of course I don't. They are sentient creatures, and you've subverted their will. It is wicked." He then looked at her. "You are under arrest by the authority of the Coalition of Known Worlds. You will—"

She let out a throaty laugh. There was a part of him that enjoyed the sound of it. But, he pushed it away. "The Makay are—"

"The Makay are barely intelligent. They still believe in gods," she said with a sigh. "It is better to take on those roles and guide them, and use them for our own aims." She let out a sigh as she knelt to look at Rick eye-to-eye. Her eyes were sea-foam green, with slitted black pupils like a cat. "Come with me, beloved. You will see it is for the best. I am Al'Kara, of the Golgoro."

The scheme was a simple one that Rick had learned about. The

Golgoro, with their strange mind powers, could subvert large groups of people. The saurians, led by Thrane, were immune to their powers. It was the reason the two species warred on Mars. Though the Science Corp believed the Golgoro were an alien race from beyond the Known Worlds.

"What are you doing here so far from your kingdom?"

"I had to leave, beloved. That is all you need to know for now."

She shook her head. "If only this helmet was off, you would—"

"Be your little toy," Rick said. "Hence I will never take it off while you are close."

The Golgoro woman looked hurt, genuinely hurt by his words. *She is a snake, don't trust that face.* Though, she was comely.

She opened her mouth to say something, but instead barked out an order in some strange tongue, her eyes going beyond Rick's head.

His suit translated it to "Incoming!" A moment before a blast knocked him against the bonds. He felt the cords cut into his suit and his own flesh and he let out a grunt of pain. He turned to see a skimmer, the kind used by the Golgoro and the Green Martians, flying over him. Three of the four-armed brutes landed, swinging their long broadswords and axes against the small, furred Makay.

The Makay squealed and shrieked, attacking the Green Martians en masse. The Golgoro went to her throne and sat upon it. She grasped the arms of the throne, and there was a *buzz* that infiltrated the suit's protection and made Rick's head pulse with a pain.

"Beloved, they are here to kill me. You have to save me. You are a Space Ranger," she said from behind him.

"I can't do anything while—"

He stopped as he felt most of his bonds were cut by something. He turned to see no blade in her hand. *Is she a psi-blade? That would explain why she is not part of the Kingdom.* A bolt from one of the saurians made Rick forget about the woman for a moment.

Rick snapped free of his last few bonds, snatching up the Tellic ray pistol. He brought it to bear on the lead saurian. It hissed and reared up to its seven-foot height. He screeched in the strange language of the Green Martians before trying to run him through with a blade. Rick's ray pistol was faster. It collapsed, and he felt the body of Al'Kara wrap around him.

"I told you you would be my beloved," she whispered. Her hands wandering over his suit. "You are such a brave man to—"

"I am not. I am simply saving you from a threat. You are still under arrest."

"Of course, beloved."

He grabbed her wrist and pulled her along behind him as they ran from the raid of the Green Martians. The Makay would be slaughtered. Even with Al'Kara safe, he needed to save as many of the smaller creatures as he could.

At the entryway to the building, he stopped and shouted out in the Common Martian tongue, "Challenge!" *This should work. It has to work. I have to save as many as possible.*

The quiet was abrupt and stunning.

"Beloved, that is—"

"I will be fine, Al'Kara," he said, holding his hand up.

The Green Martian smirked and tossed Rick a thick-headed, long axe. "Challenge accepted," the brute said, and charged.

Rick barely had time to grab it and swing. He was not well-versed in these cumbersome weapons and tripped. It saved him from being skewed by the sword of the saurian. On the next attack, Rick brought up the long haft to block the blow. Yet, he had forgotten about the four limbs of the Green Martians, and while the top two held the sword, locking the haft of his axe in place to block, the smaller arms struck out and punched Rick hard in the chest.

His weakened state from the blow earlier, along with the additional blows, hit hard enough to cause Rick's arms to buckle. The sword's pommel came down hard onto the joining of Rick's shoulder and his helm. The suit absorbed enough of the blow to not cause death, but he was knocked unconscious by the blow.

―――――

Rick came to to find Al'Kara kneeling over him. Her hands were cool to the touch on his face. *Wait! My face...I can feel...*He raised a hand to his chin, realizing his suit had been removed. Somehow, the greens had shucked him of his suit like an oyster. He was in his standard uniform of blue and red, but nothing protected him from the Golgoro mind powers or anything else. His Tellic though, was somehow still by his side. He took it up, looking at her.

Fighting a rising panic in his chest, he asked, "What is going on?" *Take a moment, Ranger, breathe.*

"You were captured by Thrane's raiding party. They took us to a fortress a half-day from the City of White Stone."

"And, how is the Tellic still here?" He felt the grip was firm, and the green light flicked on, meaning it was ready to fire. "Are you—"

"Beloved, I swear I have done nothing with your mind. I was able to fool the green beasts that it wasn't working, and they tossed it aside. I was able to secret it away. It has been waiting here this whole time. For you, beloved."

Rick didn't trust her. He didn't know if he could trust anything he was seeing. Not with the Golgoro standing there and him without his helmet. "How did they get the suit off?"

"Thrane has some new device. He was able to peel you out of it. Yet, he wishes to prepare his war council before he goes to use the suit on your ship," Al'Kara said. "We still have time—"

"He will have to do more than prepare. The ship is deadlocked. There is no way he can get in." *Yet that is also what they said about the suit. One problem at a time.* Glancing at her, he realized he'd need her help. "Do you *swear* to not use your powers on me?"

"What do you—"

"I mean, swear by your ancestors and your powers that you will not use your powers to enslave my mind." That was a little bit he remembered from the endless lectures about the Golgoro. Their oaths were strange and strong. "If you make them swear by their power, they are forced to keep it," one of his instructors said.

Al'Kara took a deep breath a look of pain on her face. "You do not *know* what you ask."

"I think I do," rick said. He didn't point the Tellic at her, but it was still ready to fire if she tried something. "Will you do it?"

"First, you will do something for me."

Rick cocked his head to the side. "What?"

"If you make a water pact with me, I will swear by my power, if you still think that is needed."

Rick paused a moment. *She would have gost towards me.* Rick knew a little of the water pact and the strange customs of honor that the tribes and people of Mars used. All the tribes except for the Green Martians, who had a different set of customs that were mostly about the strong ruling the weak. "Very well," Rick said.

He watched as she took a small bowl of water from near the door of the prison. He took in his surroundings finally and saw that the prison was spacious, strewn with some kind of rush-like material that did little more than make more of a mess. At least there was a small screen built to one side for the privy and two elevated planks for sleeping.

Al'Kara returned, and Rick realized she still wore next to nothing and tried not to stare at her.

"Are you ashamed of my body?"

"No, aren't you cold?"

"The Golgoro are use to the low temperatures of Mars. I am not cold at all, beloved."

Rick wanted her to stop using that word, yet he didn't see it happening. Al'Kara offered him a bowl of water. He took a long sip of the tepid water. "May we share water, sweat, and food."

Al'Kara took the bowl, tipped it to her lips and swallowed, then said, "And may we bond over blood and salt as well."

Rick nodded and was about to say something when Al'Kara stopped him with a look, grabbing his hand and keeping him where he was. "So mote it be," she said, then looked at him.

"So mote it be," he said, a little confused.

"Old custom. One you should know, beloved."

"Thank you." He took a breath to look at her. "And, now for your oath to me."

Al'kara bowed her head low. "Very well, beloved. I want you to trust me." He saw a small tear roll down her cheek. She started to mutter something in her native tongue, then switched to Common, "By my powers, by my ancestors, I swear I will not use my powers against you to cause harm, alter your memories, or make you see things that aren't there."

Rick nodded, "Good. Now we need to get out of here."

"How?"

"Well, how many—"

Before he finished, the door rattled as a key was thrust into the ancient metal lock. He raised his Tellic, "Or we can improvise." He pushed himself up and hid as best he could against the wall next to the door. The door opened, and a green, scaly head hove into view, the Green moved into the cell. Rick held the Tellic up, then heard a cry from Al'Kara. She had drawn her belt knife and was chanting something at the Green Martian. Halted by the Golgoro's tactic, Rick grabbed the saurial Martian and pulled in to the side.

Caught off-guard, the Green tumbled in. Rick spun to one side to avoid the creature falling onto him. Bowls of broth went flying as Rick went for the door. He heard Al'Kara shout and saw her form lunge towards the downed Martian, dagger raised high.

Outside, he saw a stunned Green looking at him with his lizard-like, green-gold eyes, the slit of his pupil shocked open in surprise. The Martian went for his blade on his hip, but Rick snapped off a shot with the Tellic. There was as shout of warning from Al'Kara in the cell. Rick spun and ducked as a third Martian from behind him sliced the air where his head was a moment before. Rick came out of his roll, the Tellic up, and fired, yet The Martian was already stilled by Al'Kara's blade in the creature's throat.

He stood and gave her a smile. She looked at him, her visage changing to a mask of hate as she charged towards him, her mouth forming strange words of the native Martian tongue. Her wet blade glinting in the torchlight of the cell.

He was about to shout, "Your oath," she pushed past him to dispatch the Green that Rick thought he had taken down with his

Tellic. She turned, snapping her blade-hand down and wiping off the worst of the dark blood with momentum, scowling at him.

"Had you not bound my powers, I would have been able to shield you from the blow."

Recovering, Rick looked at her and then at the saurial. His Tellic had taken the Martian in the side, not the killing blow he thought it had been. "I...I thank you for your help."

"Is that all you have to say, beloved?" She asked, moving a little closer to him, hand reaching out to his.

He pulled himself away from her. "Yes. We need to go before more come to investigate."

The two crept through the ancient stone fortress, surprised that they didn't encounter more of the Green Martians. Neither of them knew where to go, and after a few twists and turning corridors, found themselves next to one of the walls of the fortress. They overlooked the vast Tharsis Plains. The light of Deimos and Phobos were but small dots of light amongst a backdrop of stars. Rick was able to pick out Earth and Jupiter in the sky.

"Beloved, what is that sound?"

Rick turned to listen, hearing a *thunk-thunk-thunk* coming closer and closer. "It sounds like a sentinel of some kind. It would make sense, since there don't seem to be many of the Greens guarding this fortress."

The two pushed themselves against the cold stone of the fortress, waiting. Rick gripped the Tellic ray pistol in a tight grip. Al'Kara was holding her dagger low, her breath coming slow and constant. *She knows how to handle herself.* He felt his head wanting to take more of her in when he heard the *thunk thunk thunk* of a robotic sentinel closing. He didn't know what kind of sentinel it was. Regardless, if it was one employed by the Greens, then it would be tough and would have few weak spots.

A long heartbeat later, the thing crested the last of the steps the pair had just ascended. It was a pale, pearl color, with a squat head and a single, glowing, red eye. Four arms moved in a constant rotation along its cylindrical body. Each arm was tipped by a pinching claw that looked curved and sharp. The feet were thick, flat, round appendages, and bore the sentinel forward in a short, lumbering steps.

He took a deep breath of the thin air and hoped and prayed that he hit the sentinel in the first salvo. Otherwise, he'd be torn limb from limb. The fair Al'Kara waited next to him, her personal blade in hand. He didn't want to tell her that against the sentinel, it would be useless. She closed her hand tight, a pale sheen shimmered around her fist and there was a translucent blade.

Rick swallowed hard. "You are a psi-blade?" He'd heard of them, yet he was stunned to be so close to one in the flesh. They were rumored to be crazed mystics who extolled an ancient religion and were fanatically devout.

"Yes beloved. And, now you must know that the oath you had me take could cause problems."

Rick looked at her, "No, it will protect me from your powers."

Al'Kara shook her head. She then leaned in close and stole a kiss before Rick could pull away. "Beloved, you are so charming for a simple man. You will find out in time why it was a bad idea."

The sentinel rounded the corner, its bulbous head and bright, multifaceted eyes glowing in the dim twilight of the planet. Rick sprang forward, his pistol shooting out three fluorescent green rays. They struck true. The sentinel reeled backwards. One of its arms snapped forward, grabbing at Rick's shoulder. In its last moments, the claw-like hand gripped his shoulder and dug into bone and flesh. Rick felt intense pain and the pressure of his bones grating on each other. He felt himself being pulled over the edge of the small wall that he and the sentinel were atop. The weight of the sentinel caused more pain to lance through Rick's unprotected shoulder.

Al'Kara let out a high-pitched wail, striking from her position and jamming the blade, which was a startling florescent green, of her dagger into the joints of the wrist of the hand that dragged Rick down. There was a smell of ozone and a few errant sparks, and the clawed appendage's weight went slack. The sentinel fell away without the clawed hand, which remained in Rick's shoulder. Al'Kara looked at him.

"I told you, beloved. It would come in handy." She pulled him close to give him a kiss. He embraced her, and for a moment, it was only the two of them on the wall, in the ancient castle, on the planet Mars. For a brief moment, his training failed him. He pulled away from the kiss, reluctantly. Her lips were warm and inviting. *No, she is your prisoner. Stop that! You can't get involved. You have a mission to complete.* "We should go," Rick said, pulling away from her. He tried to ignore the look of pain in her eyes.

"Very well, Ranger. Lead on." She pulled away from him, head dropping.

He didn't know why, but when she used the formal title, he felt a sting deeper than the claw in his shoulder.

Al'Kara did what she could, binding the wound and applying water from Rick's small canteen that was part of his uniform, yet it still hurt. Rick pushed through the pain, and the two went deeper into the dark fortress. Through luck, guile, and the Golgoro mental trickery, the pair found their way to the outside of the treasure vault without further incident. There, two Black Martian slave-soldiers waited, their thick-bladed polearms and simple belts and arm-bound shields marked them as slave-soldiers of the Thrane. Their wide, flat faces leered into the dark hallway with large, multifaceted eyes that glinted in the wan light from the torches along the wall.

"Beloved, we must leave," she whispered, pulling him by his injured shoulder.

He grunted in pain and pulled away. "Al'Kara, I need to get my suit. Without it, I'll never survive the rocket ride home."

"We can escape to my homeland."

"I must get to my rocket before Thrane." He touched her shoulders and smiled. "I understand if—"

Before he could finish, she slipped from his hands and slid into the shadows. "If you won't be sensible, then wait here," she said with a scoff, then was gone. Her voice at the end was muffled by something, but Rick wasn't sure what.

Dimly, at the end of the hallway, he watched the two slave soldiers, their heads scanning the area around them in constant sweeping arcs. Rick checked the power level of his Tellic, seeing it still had about half power. *Will I have enough to get out of here, or will I have to use it on everything I come across?* The idea of using his Tellic not as a means of defense, but to wantonly kill, terrified him. To be nothing but a murderous human, like his ancient forebears. *To be no better than the Thrane himself. No. Never!*

He was pulled from his thoughts when he heard a strange humming sound. The noise drew the attention of the two soldiers at the vault. Rick noticed a distortion in the dark hallway. There was a shadow the guardians didn't, or couldn't, see. He concentrated on the distortion and felt his heart hammer in his chest. The shape was vaguely of a human. *Al'Kara.* Somehow invisible and striding toward the two guards without being detected.

He narrowed his eyes to focus on the distortion as it grew closer and closer to the two Black Martians. The two soldiers didn't see what was coming, yet their cunning and feral instincts detected something. Their polearms whirled into a defensive posture, their strange multi-hinged jaws worked in a constant, chewing-like motion with spittle oozing from the split in their chins to dribble down to the floor. Rick levelled his Tellic at the two, hoping he would be able to hit them and not the beauty who had helped him escape.

There was a flash of light, and he was momentarily blinded by the light. He heard the hissing shriek of the two guards, letting him know they were blinded as well. Then there was the undulating cry of Al'Kara and the sound of a blade cutting through sinew and bone, followed by the wet sound of a dead body hitting the hard stone floor. He blinked away, bright spots in his vision, and saw the form of Al'Kara standing before the two dead guards.

"Beloved, hurry," she shouted.

He joined her and gave a look at the vault door. "How are we going to—"

Al'Kara stepped forward and tapped several runes on the vault's convex metal hatch. Each rune glowed with a faint blue light. When she touched the fifth one, the light changed to a turquoise, and the hatch popped open with a faint *click* and then swung open on noiseless hinges.

Rick was about to ask how she knew when he was distracted by the sights inside. Piles of gold and jewels in mounds as tall as Rick were artfully arranged around the edges of the vault, many of them under sets of armor for the Green Martians, with elongated breastplates, and some with multiple sets of arm vambraces, and a few that had to be Golgoro battle-wear of brass, bronze, and gold.

In the center was the vermillion-and-gold suit of the Space Rangers, the helm set upon the suit, but askew and not locked onto the suit. Rick took a step forward. He heard, too late, Al'Kara shout out a warning as the vault door slammed shut, and he was plunged into darkness.

Looking around, the only light was the dimly glowing sigil of the Space Rangers on his suit. He took a step forward, swallowing hard.

"Are you afraid?" The voice of the Thrane echoed through the enclosed chamber.

"A Ranger faces their fear," Rick snapped back, reciting part of the code.

"Then, we shall see how well you can face it!"

Lights ignited in the vault. Rick snapped his eyes closed, trying to banish the ugly flowers and pain from the sudden brightness. When he opened them, his suit was gone from the center of the vault. Instead, it stood several steps from him, besides the plinth, with Thrane inside it. "Come and fight me, Ranger! We will see who is worthy of the suit!"

The helmet of the suit rolled away from Thrane, who was not able to latch it shut around his snout. *At least he isn't completely sealed up. I have a chance.*

Rick charged forward, breaking off at the last second to roll behind a pillar as the Thrane lashed out with a long-hafted spear. Coming up from the roll, Rick fired three times, aiming for the Thrane's head. None struck, each one blocked by the haft of the spear.

"You will never win that way," Thrane snarled. He whirled the spear overhead, charging as he did. His legs didn't move well in the suit, but it would protect him from the Tellic blasts. Rick fired at the Martian's face again. Each time, the spear blocked it.

Thrane let out another laugh. Rick dove behind a pile of gold and a Golgoro battle harness as the Thrane flung a spear at him. Rick felt trapped. *How am I supposed to get around this? He's in the suit. He's armored. His face is exposed, but I can't get a clear shot of it. How...*

He shook his head, realizing what he was doing wrong. He popped out from behind the pile of gold, levelling the Tellic at Thran's chest, right at the glowing rune of the Rangers. He fired, again and again. Thrane didn't try to block, letting out a long laugh. He charged Rick, hurling another spear at the ranger. At the last minute, he dove out of the way, firing until the last second at the legs and the chest again.

The Thrane threw a vicious backhand, catching Rick as he tried to raise his weapon. The Tellic went spinning off in one direction. Thrane tried to grab at Rick, but then the arm locked up.

"You see Thrane, the problem you have is that you had to much faith in the suit, like I did." Rick walked over to the still form of Thrane, who was cursing in Martian as Rick leaned down. "The suit can only take so much damage." Rick touched the suit, which started to break open like an egg. He pointed one of the tossed spears at Thrane's neck. "I have won, get out."

"No, you will have to kill me."

"I am not going to kill you. I can't."

"Then, you will die," Thrane snarled, his right arm snapped up, wrapping around Rick's throat. "Humans are so weak. You can't—"

Thrane's words were lost as Rick jabbed the spear into Thrane's armpit. As the hand relaxed, Thrane looked at him quizzically.

"I can't kill you in cold blood, but defending myself is a different story."

Limping to his feet, he pulled the suit off Thrane. He scooped up the helmet with one hand and looked at the entrance to the vault. There, Al'Kara stood, taken prisoner by the Green Martians. They looked at Rick aghast.

"They want to know what you wish to do with me," Al'Kara said. "You are their leader. What shall it be, beloved?"

Ten minutes later, Rick was on the deck of a skimmer, still trying to stand up. Al'Kara was piloting the thing away from the fortress and the ensuing chaos. Without Thrane, and without Rick to lead them, the Green Martians were fighting amongst themselves already, a small civil war between three different groups. "This assignment is going to kill me," Rick mused, watching the fortress grow smaller and smaller.

"What was that, beloved?"

Rick looked up at Al'Kara in a new light. She was not the vile, scheming creature he had thought. She was taking advantage of the Makay, but that would stop once he got her back to her people. His suit would need some time before it could fully repair itself.

"Beloved, come and watch the scenery."

"What about the Thrane's forces?"

"They will not catch us," she said. She reached out, and Rick took her hand, smiling at her as he stood. He watched the scenery pass and smiled. "I said, I think this assignment is going to kill me."

"You will be able to rest in Golgoro."

"I had to go there anyway. Still, who knows what will happen there."

Rick and Al'Kara flew over the red-orange soil of the lower Tharsis plains. The flitter's cramped quarters pressed Al'Kara against him. She whispered in his ear, "You have freed me, beloved. You shall be rewarded richly when we reach the kingdom of Golgoro. You will live like a king."

"But what about my assignment? I have the rest of the Solar System to go through before I get an assignment."

She looked at him. "Would I be able to go with you?"

"Rangers usually go alone. Or rarely, in teams."

"So, you would leave me?"

Rick pulled her closer. "I said usually. There might be a way." He lied to her too easily, and it didn't feel right, but he needed to prepare her, just in case. He *did* have an assignment to follow through on. On the other hand, the suit needed repair, and he needed some rest. He pushed these thoughts aside and let the warmth of Al'Kara comfort him for the moment. He could think about the assignment later.

"It is a pretty landscape." He said, looking right at her.

She smiled back and kissed him. He didn't pull away.

PART TWO

R ick's suit worked enough that it didn't lock up when he put it on. The smell of the Thrane's body, a musty, oily residue, had been expunged thanks to the suit's filtering system, but still, something felt off. He continued to wear his helmet, even though Al'Kara said he wouldn't need it. "I feel safer with it on," he said. Rick did *feel* more secure, looking towards the Golgoro Moot with his helmet on. Al'Kara had already gotten off the skimmer on the mesa outside of the Moot. They had stopped well outside the boundary of the meeting grounds. Al'Kara said the mesa would give them a good vantage point to give Rick a "first look" at the Golgoro Moot. She said it was the closest they could get before being detected.

Catching a glimpse of the Moot from where they stood, Rick felt his body tremble at the sight. So many Golgoro in one place. Seeing that many, without his suit at full strength? He was without the full-powered suit for protection. A part of him felt shamed. His suit was still damaged from the fight with the Thrane, and it felt wrong on him, as if he didn't deserve it. After a moment, he finally peeled it off and left it in the skimmer.

Rick felt as though he was a weak Space Ranger, unable to do more than wield his Tellic and hide behind the authority of the Rangers.

Even the Golgoro were touchy about the Ranger's authority on Mars. By the time he reached Al'Kara, he was startled at the sheer number of people and tents that carpeted the plains of Tharsis before him. From one side of the wide plain to the other, stretching from horizon to horizon, he saw the colourful tents and the red-skinned Golgoro, who were walking around the vast Tharsis Plains along with their beasts of burden, carts, or both. They moved around the paths and routes between the varied set-ups of tent "districts," which was the best word he could think of for what he witnessed.

"Beloved, what is wrong?" Al'Kara asked, touching his arm.

The touch shook him from his thoughts, so he turned towards her. "I had no idea that there were this many Golgoro in one spot," he said, gesturing towards the massive tent city. There were thousands upon thousands of tents, large and small. Pack animals of all kinds wandered in and around the massive tent city, paths, and larger routes that looked like thoroughfares between large blocks of tents spread out before them. "What is this place?" He asked.

"It is the Moot, beloved." She then moved a little closer to him. "It is held once a lifetime. Is there something wrong with it?" She asked, a look of concern scrunching up her face.

"The Space Rangers will need to know that there are so many tribes of the Golgoro. There are banners I've never seen before," he said, going to his gauntlet and starting to take notes with a series of keystrokes.

"Why?" Al'Kara asked, pulling her hand away. "Why tell the Rangers?"

"They want to keep tabs on those of Mars, like every planet. We are peacekeepers, Al'Kara. We need to know it all," Rick said, waving his hands at the giant tent city. "If we don't have accurate notes—"

"So you can control us?" Al'kara's spine went rigid, staring at him. He noticed a vague blue-black aura around her for a heartbeat, but ignored it as a trick of the light.

Rick looked at her, confused. "No, so we can keep the *peace*. That is what we do."

"Space Rangers do more than keep the peace," Al'Kara whispered. "You yourself came close to killing me."

"You were controlling the Makay. You used them as puppets and toys," Rick said, shuddering slightly while remembering the horrific ordeal in the City of Lotus.

"Only to get your attention," Al'Kara said with a smirk.

"What?" His hand dropped to his Tellic. He snatched his hand away. *Not the right response. She made a pact. We're…*allies.

"A bad joke," she said, her eyes not missing where his hand was before he jerked it away. She raised an eyebrow but said nothing for a moment. "I *am* sorry. I wish I could tell you why I was there. Some kind of force made me do it. I can only tell you that."

She had said this before, once they were away from Thrane's fortress. He didn't know what to believe at the moment. "What stopped you from hurting me in prison? Or controlling me if *it* controlled you?" Rick asked, unnerved by her confession.

"When I awoke in the cell with you, I felt as though I was whole again. Something had used part of my mind, beloved. I swear to you." She grabbed his hands and kissed them. "I swear, I am nothing like that woman from Lotus." She kissed his hands again.

I want to believe her. Rick didn't know if he could. He had made the pact with her in the cell in the fortress out of a need for an ally. He also knew that she was bound to him by that pact. *Are her thoughts on gost and mydel enough to trust her?* He swallowed, looking at her. "You can't read my mind, can you?" He still wasn't sure if it was a lie.

"No, beloved. I swore a water pact with you. I cannot use it. You know that." She cocked her head to the side. "Do you think I would lie after a pact?"

"I don't know." Rick pulled away from her, moving along the mesa's edge. He ran his hands through his hair, feeling frustration and anger boil inside him. He *had* a simple mission. Come to Mars, do his patrol, and *leave*. Since he had chosen to go off-mission that moment —*that one moment*—in Lotus was when everything went wrong. He could only imagine what would happen when he got back to the rocket, and his suit automatically uploaded its intel. *I'm going to be booted from the Rangers for sure— If I* even get back *to the rocket.* He felt a hand on his shoulder. He turned to see Al'Kara smiling up at him.

"Beloved, you have to trust me," Al'Kara said, moving closer to him while sliding her hand to his.

"How can I trust you?" He asked. He didn't resist taking her hand this time.

She pulled back as if slapped. She pulled away from him and looked at the tent city. "Did the fortress teach you *nothing*?" Her voice was tight.

Rick realized what she said and felt the stinging rebuke for what it was. He was being a child, a petulant child. Ranger Command might have its own thoughts on what was going on on Mars, but he had seen what was really going on. The Golgoro could teach him something that he could bring back to Command, *something* that could help them and their mission to protect the system. Also, he did know ways to keep the suit from making a full report during his pre-flight before blasting off to Callisto. *When* he reached the rocket.

He turned back to Al'Kara. "I am sorry, I've had a long—"

Some of her rigidity diminished. "You've had a long few days, beloved. I wish you would stop sleeping away from me. I can help you in ways you can't even—"

Rick felt his cheeks burn a little. "I think we need to cross that bridge when we come to it. Let's go down and join in. You said I would welcomed, is that right?" He asked, hoping to change the subject.

He saw Al'Kara give him a sad smile. She then gave him a small smile as she looked towards her people. "Yes, the Golgoro *will* accept you as long as you come as my guest. Or as my—"

Rick waved her to stop. "I know, Al'Kara. I have regulations to deal with. A guest is adequate for what we need."

There was a shifting on her face, her smile turning hard. "What do we *need*, beloved?"

"Time for the suit to fully charge. To talk to some of the heads of the Golgoro and then leave." He didn't say, "I leave," but he wanted to.

"As you say, beloved." Al'Kara said, pulling away and starting to walk down the steep switchback-laden trail that cut into the mesa towards the main entrance of the tent city. Rick ducked back to the skimmer to put his suit back on and then joined her in her descent. She gave him a disgusted look when she saw him above her in the suit. She said nothing and kept on walking.

"It will not be looked upon kindly here, even if you are my guest," Al'Kara said, indicating the suit and helmet. She then shrugged. "If you wish to keep it on."

"But it will be tolerated?" Rick asked.

"For a time," she said, not looking at him as she entered the throng of people that waited at the main entrance of the massive tent city. As soon as someone saw her, they moved to the side, creating a gap large enough for her and Rick to walk through without either of them being touched. The looks the assembled Golgoro gave Rick were a mixture of confusion, anger, and disgust, but they did nothing, seeing that he traveled with Al'Kara. A few Golgoro crossed their fingers, then crossed their wrists over their chests upon seeing Rick, giving him an angry sneer until disappearing into the throng around him.

Two tall, muscular Golgoro guarded the entrance, a gate five meters tall that took up twenty meters of the massive fence that surrounded the edges of the tent city. The guards were called wands-men, according to Al'Kara. Essentially they were the militia and civil guard of the Moot. They took their orders from the High Chief Council, yet they had their own latitude, Al'Kara had warned. Both held brass wands, thirty-five to forty centimeters in length. Each was capped by two silver balls on either end. Both the silver balls and brass length glinted in the weak light of the distant sun. Their skin was a darker, more baked-brick color than Al'Kara's own flesh, and their dark eyes glanced past Al'Kara to stare with murderous intent on Rick.

"What is the Earth Man doing here, psi-blade Kara?" One of the wandsman asked.

"He's my guest, Ba'hal," she said, a touch of venom in her voice. Rick didn't miss the aura around her hands turn visible, a dark blue radiating from her clenched fists at her sides.

The other wandsman held out his arm to pull back Ba'hal. "We are sorry, Al'Kara." He then looked at Rick. "But, he is a Ranger…they—"

Al'Kara took a step forward, her hands flattening out, the nimbus growing sharper to a small point a few centimeters beyond her middle finger. "He is my *guest*. He is to be offered *guest rights*," Al'Kara said through clenched teeth.

"Yes, Psi Blade Al'Kara," they both said, pulling away from her and Rick. Rick noticed even the other Golgoro near them backed up half a step from Al'Kara's words.

"Please, enter," Ba'hal said, gesturing towards the open gate. His eyes still glared at Rick with anger.

As they entered, Rick moved closer. "What are guest rights?" He whispered to his companion.

Al'Kara cut him an annoyed look as she moved, pulling him through the gate. He didn't resist. "Anything you do reflects on me. Anything done to you is an assault on myself, and by extension, the psi-blade Temple."

"I thought that was some myth?"

Al'Kara let out a small laugh. "A myth?" She revealed her hands still encased in the blue aura. "Does this look like a myth, beloved?"

Rick swallowed. "No."

With a smile, she moved forward, and Rick followed.

Once they left the main entrance, he was in awe of what he saw. Tents of every possible color, the sizes ranging from small little single-occupant tents to large ones that would rival Barnum and Bailey's. And there were even large ones he glimpsed as the pair moved closer to the interior.

"What is this city for, what is this Moot for?" Rick asked, stunned by the sheer number of Golgoro. They ranged from young to old, male and female, in a variety of colors from ochre, to brick, to brilliant vermillion. Some had skin carvings, others had tattoos, and still others whose skin was covered in paints or whorls and symbols. There were hawkers of all stripes and merchants. He saw tradesman in glass, jewellery, and weapons. He saw mercenaries roving around with weapons that looked ancient, as well as a few walking around with long arm ray guns that unsettled him. He kept his mind on following Al'Kara.

"Once a generation, the Golgoro come to make treaties, trade goods, and make new clan laws and elect new clan leaders," Al'Kara said without stopping.

"Yet, you interact at other times?"

"Yes, many on a daily basis. But, *this*," she said, gesturing to the tent city itself, "is something that happens once a generation. Even I see clans I've never seen before. I will meet clan members from rival clans here. And...old suitors." She stopped as she said the last few words, letting Rick catch up.

Without thinking, Rick asked, "Is that going to be a problem?"

She looked at him, a sly smile on her lips, her hips shifted towards him. "If you would listen to me more, it would not be," she said, the smile changing into a serious look. "You do have to be careful here, beloved."

"What do you mean?" Rick asked, confused.

Al'Kara shook her head. "We don't have time to discuss the reasons here, but I did tell you that it would be dangerous." She turned and continued walking.

Rick looked at her as she strode from him, deeper into the warren of the tent city. He didn't completely understand her words, yet he knew she had to been lying. She had said that as her guest, he'd be seen as a friend. "But you said I had—" He stopped when he looked up, and she was gone.

He continued beyond where he'd last seen her before being stopped short by two men with dark swirls and whorls of black around their cheeks and chest. Each hefted a short, spiked club and a familiar wand thrust through their leather belt.

"What is your business here, stranger?" One of the wandsmen said, shifting his hand to his wand.

"I am here at the behest of Al'Kara," Rick said.

Both of the wandsmen stared at him. "You mean Kara of the Psi-Blade? You will respect her with her full name." The first wandsman said, grabbing at Rick's arm.

Rick's instincts kicked in. As the wandsman grabbed at him, he pushed himself backwards. The gravity of Mars allowed him to leap back several feet into the startled crowd. The Golgoro scattered when he landed. Rick watched the two wandsmen moving forward, their wands held out with menace, their faces set with anger.

"An Earthman," the first wandsman said with a sneer, looking ready to strike at Rick.

"A Ranger," the other said, pointing at the suit. His club was in one hand and the wand in the other, both looking to be comfortable in the guard's hand.

Rick swallowed hard, trying to keep from grasping his Tellic. He stayed clear of the two wandsmen, continuing to move and duck out of reach. Each time, he tried to get around them, attempting to escape to where Al'Kara had vanished. He pulled away from them in a dodge that brought the two of them together. He made it two meters before his suit locked up for a crucial moment, his momentum stopped hard. As his suit started to move again, a heavy hand fell on Rick's shoulder from behind. "You're not—"

Training kicked in for Rick again. He grabbed the hand, thrusting his hip backwards to gain leverage and threw the man over his shoulder. The throw was hard, and there was a bone-wrenching *pop* that came from the wandsman's shoulder as he landed.

"What is the meaning of this?" a rough voice shouted from Rick's left, stunning everyone, including Rick.

Rick turned to see that an older, imposing Golgoro stepped forward. His dark hair was streaked with gray, and he was one of the few darker Golgoro with facial hair, a short well-trimmed goatee that was flecked with gray as well. He wore a long cloak of gray, silk-like material. The portion of his chest that was revealed was covered in a thin shirt of off-green, and his pants were a darker gray. His eyes were green; not just the iris, the entire eye was bathed in jade. As Rick focused, he realized that there was a soft green aura around him.

The man with all-green eyes stared at Rick. "What is an Earthman Ranger doing here in the Moot?" He roared the question. The words forced Rick to one knee. He caught glimpses of the entire crowd being driven to one knee. Even the wandsmen knelt.

Al'Kara appeared from out the crowd, "He is with me, Uncle. He is my guest."

The green-eyed Golgoro turned to regard Al'Kara. "You would bring a *stranger* to the Moot? A *Ranger* of all things?" Al'Kara's uncle curled his lip. "He injured a wandsman."

"After he put hands on me," Rick said. He looked up to see Al'Kara's uncle snap his head back to him.

"Do not *speak, Earthman!* I will—"

"Is that true?" Al'Kara asked the wandsmen on the ground, ignoring her uncle. The wandsman still nursed his injured shoulder. The green-eyed Golgoro looked shocked that his niece ignored him. Rick smirked; *she would do something like that.* Several of his fellow wandsmen had appeared, all with their batons out in a semi-circle around the two wandsmen, Al'Kara, and Rick. It wasn't until then that Rick realized that the wand's two silver balls were different sizes, a thicker ball on the end held out and a smaller one where the wandsmen rested their hands.

"No," the injured wandsmen said, looking up at Rick with a rictus of pain and anger. "He attacked me without provocation."

"I would never," Rick started. "I—"

Al'Kara held her hand up. "Beloved, be quiet. We have ways of knowing."

"Are you saying that the wandsman's word is a lie, Al'Kara?" Her uncle asked, his tone ice.

Al'Kara looked at Rick and swallowed hard. He could see that she was torn. Rick wanted to say something, but Al'Kara held up her hand as he tried to open his mouth. "Yes, Uncle. The wandsman is lying," she said. Her eyes flickered to Rick a moment, then turned and faced her uncle.

A muttering sprang up from the crowd that had surrounded the small cluster of wandsmen, Rick, Al'Kara, and her uncle. Her uncle swept a hand over the crowd and there was silence. Rick felt a soft hum in the helm, and he realized the man had just tried to use some kind of mental attack on him and the rest of the crowd. Rick's hand dropped to the Tellic, but only rested on it. *I have to trust Al'Kara. She knows what she is doing.* He knew that if he tried to do anything with his ray gun, he'd be causing more problems, both for Al'Kara and himself. *And it was already looking grim.*

The uncle glared at Rick for a long moment, and Rick thought the Golgoro man *wanted* him to pull the Tellic. *That is an insane thought. Stop thinking that all the Golgoro are the enemy. Al'Kara isn't. She is...more. So gentle and yet...*He stopped himself from continuing that line of thought. It wasn't professional to think of her like that.

"This needs to be held in a Guild Tent," Al'Kara said, looking at her uncle.

He glared at her, then nodded. Two wandsmen and the injured one followed Al'Kara and her uncle. Al'Kara beckoned Rick to follow along as well. The rest of the crowd slowly dispersed.

They entered a large tent of red and gold. The tent was large enough to easily accommodate all of the assembled group as well as at least ten more people without having a hard time finding a place to sit and or stand. Rick tried to get closer to Al'Kara, but two men in similar garb to Al'Kara's uncle waited inside the tent as the wandsmen pushed him away bodily from Al'Kara. Rick knew he could overcome them with the suit, but he let them stop him. *Trust Al'Kara. You've no other choice.*

Her uncle wheeled on her when all were assembled. "Al'Kara, what *is* the meaning of allowing guest rights for an *Earthman!* The vileness of his presences causes the Twins to weep."

Al'Kara stood her ground. "He helped me, Uncle. He saved me from the Thrane. Please, Cal'Bain, he—"

"*He* helped you? A psi-blade needed the help of an *Earthman?*" Cal'bain interrupted at the same time, here was a moment of shocked looks traded amongst the rest of the gathered people at Al'Kara's words.

"Yes, Uncle. I was on a mental quest." Rick kept his head down, ignoring the lie from Al'Kara, hoping she would explain later. "The Thrane and his forces overwhelmed me. I awoke to find Rick Tavish.

Neither of us could escape alone. I made a water pact with him." All eyes went to Rick. "And then we helped each other escape."

Cal'Bain cleared his throat, and Rick looked to him. "Is this true, Earthman?"

"Yes," Rick said, He felt a small twinge from lying. Yet it wasn't *all* a lie. At least he tried to tell himself that.

There was a moment of silence as Cal'Bain looked from Al'Kara to Rick and back, looking as though he was weighing their words. Finally, he asked, "And you gave him guest rights when you entered the Moot?"

Al'Kara ducked her head. "Yes, Uncle."

There was a much longer pause this time. Cal'Bain looked like he was mulling things over for some time. Rick felt himself twitch a little. He opened his mouth to speak when Cal'Bain spoke again.

"You disappoint me, Kara. I *am* glad you are safe. And this *human* will be given guest rights. I would have liked to make him remove his Ranger helm so I could probe his mind. However, that is not possible thanks to his right."

"He's to be kept separate from the rest of the Temple. You will be the only one allowed to interact with him."

"Yes, Uncle," Al'Kara said with a small nod.

Cal'Bain's frown softened. He moved closer to her. "It *is* good to see you, little blade." He took her in his arms and gave her a hug.

"It is good to see you too, Stone," Al'Kara said, returning the hug with warmth.

Her uncle then pushed her away. "Please go and attend to him. I must settle the issue with the wandsman for the Temple, since the wandsman attacked someone under our protection," he said, giving Rick a hard look.

"Yes, Uncle," Al'Kara said, pulling Rick from a stupor into another portion of the tent. He followed without saying anything as they entered a partitioned section of the tent. Rick found it strange that when Al'Kara dropped the partition back into place, the noise from the main part of the tent went silent. He looked at the partition material, confused.

"How is that—"

"It is woven from a specific plant and treated with alchemical processes to block noise, beloved. We have complete privacy here."

"Who was that?"

"My uncle. The Stone of the psi-blades. He is the leader, the one who handles disputes between members, and for certain situations, like the current one."

"Why a temple? I thought you said it wasn't all mystical hoodoo?"

Al'Kara smiled. "It is not 'hoodoo,' whatever that means. It is a place of learning of your inner self. It is a place of meditation and reflection. Most Golgoro have some form of a temple. Do you not have something like that on Earth?"

Rick looked at her and shook his head. "A few places, but a temple implies religion though, right?"

"It *was* a religion, until the Golgoro realized it was our own mental powers that allowed 'miracles' to occur form the varied prophets. It is a holdover of an older era, beloved."

"What is a psi-blade?"

"Psi-blades are not the crazy mystics that you think we are, beloved. The Psi are those of the Golgoro who can make weapons of our minds. Many of us can influence others. Yet, the Psi can do more." She closed her fist, and an aura of darkness swept over her closed fist. A blade of dark light extended from her fist. "This is one of the first things we are taught. To make a blade of our mental energy. Hence the term psi-blade."

"Why did he call you little blade?"

She snapped her head towards him. "That is a Temple name, beloved. You aren't allowed to use that. Unless..." Her face softened, and she moved closer, moving over the suit's shoulders and across his chest. "You wish to use this place of solitude for something more...amorous?"

"Not now. Please, Al'Kara. Can you at least tell me why you lied?"

"The short answer is that I don't trust the Temple. It is very possible that whoever controlled me is here. The longer answer requires more time than we have. Do you trust me?"

Rick looked at her and smiled. He let out a breath. "Yes. Yes, I do." He took her hand in his gloved one.

"Good. I will explain more later, when we are completely safe."

"We aren't now?" He asked.

"No. You wounded a wandsman. That is usually punished by death." Al'Kara let her hand slip from his grasp. "We have to wait until—"

The partition opened, and one of Cal'Bain's men poked his head in. "You and the *Earthman* are needed out here, little blade."

"Only me, Rick," Al'Kara said as she moved towards the exit.

"No, the *Earthman* as well. Cal'Bain has come up with a solution," the guard said with a smile when he looked at Rick.

When they entered the main portion of the tent, Rick saw the wounded wandsman staring at him, and he didn't look harmed at all. Before he could say anything, Cal'Bain spoke, pulling his attention.

"You have wounded a wandsman, so you must be put on trial." Cal'Bain smirked, his all-green eyes boring into Rick.

Al'Kara spoke up. "The wandsman is the one who broke the guest rights first, Cal'Bain. You can't—"

Cal'Bain swept a hand over Al'Kara, "Al'Kara, you must be tired. Please, *go rest*." Rick watched as she staggered for a moment before Cal'Bain's men took her and swept her behind the same partition of the tent the pair had left moments before. It left the tent empty save Cal'Bain, Rick, and the wandsman. Al'Kara's uncle turned his all-green eyes to Rick. "Now, we can speak as men," Cal'Bain said with a soft smirk. He turned his green eyes toward Rick. "You wounded the wandsman, Ceb. You will be put on trial for it."

Rick shook his head. "You underestimate your niece, sir. She is a strong woman and knows what she spoke of. That man broke guest rights first," Rick said, pointing his hand at Ceb, whose shoulder was now uninjured. The wandsman smirked at Rick's confusion. "However, if I am to be put on trial, I shall face it."

"Would you like to have a fair fight?"

Without thinking, "Yes." Then, Rick realized what Cal'Bain said. "Fight? You mean the trial is—"

"Ah, trial by combat it is," Cal'Bain completed Rick's words, a small smirk on his face growing brighter.

"What does a 'fair fight' involve?" Rick asked, looking from Cal'Bain to Ceb and back.

"No mental tricks from Ceb. And no help from your suit," Cal'Bain said, pointing towards Rick's suit.

Rick let out a breath he didn't know he was holding. *Wonderful. This is not going to end well.* He touched the hilt of his Tellic. "And, no ray guns, of course."

"No. Knives!" Ceb said with a fierce smile.

"Ceb is the injured party and chooses weapons and venue," Cal'Bain said.

Rick shook his head. *So much for diplomacy.* "Yes, I accept trial by combat."

There was laughter from both Ceb and Cal'Bain. "Good," they both said as one.

"What did I get myself into?" Rick muttered, more to himself than anyone else.

Rick paced in the small tent, looking out to the area that he'd seen briefly before being shoved into the small preparation tent before the trial. There was a large crowd gathering in the stands and there were cheers from them as they watched beasts from Mars' badlands. The fight between Ceb and himself was the main event, and, apparently, the bloodlust needed to be primed by the beast fights. It was warm and humid in the tent, and Rick was already sweating.

Al'Kara had left to see if she could talk her uncle out of it. Rick knew it was a fool's errand but didn't stop her. He paced around the small tent, feeling exposed without his suit. It was in the corner, a portion of it exposed to the weak sunlight outside so it would continue to charge. There was a part of him that wanted to grab it, take his chances running, and get to his rocket. His Tellic would be more than a match for any of the weapons the Golgoro had. Then, his eyes spotted a few of the wandsmen hefting longarm ray guns of their own. They were patrolling the area around the arena, and this put the thought out of his head. *It also isn't the way of the Space Rangers to run from problems.*

He settled down on the small stool that was the only piece of furniture in the tent and looked down at the dagger he had been given. It was a bone hilt with a blade made of the strange glass-like stone the Golgoro used. It was not obsidian but something like it. It was as sharp as steel and not as brittle as obsidian, since he slammed it twice into a tent pole and there was not even a chip.

Al'Kara entered, her face grim.

"Your uncle won't allow it to be stopped?"

"No, beloved. I don't understand why. It is as if he's not in right mind."

"Much like you in Lotus?"

"You don't think that—"

"I only know that something has happened on this planet. And, I can't investigate it because of the trouble I keep getting myself into."

Al'Kara came up to him, wrapping her arms around his shoulders from behind. "Was it all trouble, beloved?"

He touched her arms and smiled. "No, not all of it." It hadn't even dawned on him until she touched him. She was helping him and trying to save him, and she didn't have to. He felt that she was honest. She did care for him, and he was starting to feel the same way about her. *Dammit, Command is going to hate it, but she needs to come with me. If I win this, we will have to leave Mars.* The *if* was the issue.

"I wonder how fair the fight will really be?" Rick asked.

Al'Kara came to stand before Rick and smiled, "For my part, there is nothing I can do. You had me bind myself against using my powers on you."

Rick sighed. "I know. I suppose we can only hope that Cal'Bain will be honest as well."

"With the Temple here and so many other Golgoro? He will have to respect the pact we made, love."

Nodding, Rick took up the knife given to him by Cal'Bain. "So, can you give me any pointers? I was never a fan of using a knife." He'd already taken a few quiet moments to berate himself in private. He *had* been schooled in the basics of knife combat in the Academy, but everything from those lessons flittered out of his head the longer he tried to focus on them. Much like the way most of his training slipped away the longer he stayed on Mars. He wanted to run, flee with his suit, hide somewhere, get to the ship, and blast off. Run off from Mars and head to his next assignment. *Like a coward.*

That wasn't going to happen. He gripped the bone-hilt dagger harder and felt his shoulder ache. The old wound from the sentinel in Thrane's fortress, from what felt like years ago, was throbbing. He didn't see Al'Kara until she touched the wound on his shoulder with a cool touch. He looked up at her while she smiled down at him. He felt something cooling and soothing entering his flesh and lifting away the burning pain.

"How?" He asked, confused by what happened.

She held up her hand, revealing a small device affixed to her palm. It was a gold device with brass rings attached to the body of the device which looped over her fingers. An asymmetrical plate of dark metal with strange glowing crystals sat atop the golden disc. The glow diminished as she pulled it from his shoulder. "A healing device. Think of it as a way around our pact," she said with a wink.

"Thank you," Rick said, flexing and testing his shoulder.

"I—"

Al'Kara put her hand to his mouth. "Not now."

"Well, I—"

"Beloved, you can't run from this. You have to—"

Rick cocked an eyebrow. "You said you wouldn't use your powers on me?"

She let out a small laugh. "It is written plainly on your face. If it hadn't been for me, you would be back at your ship." Her face fell as she spoke. "It is my fault you're in this—"

"No, I made the choice to check out what was wrong at the City of Lotus. I had a gut feeling something wrong was going on there." He stood up, took her hand, and pulled her closer. "And, I have no regrets." He knew he meant it.

"None?" She asked, a small smile on her face.

"None," he said, giving her a kiss on the lips. It was a little less chaste then he thought he should give her.

He pulled away, and she gave her a bigger smile. "I am glad to hear it."

"Same...beloved," he said, turning and walking away before she could say anything to make him stay.

Outside, the sun shone down on him. The small moon of Phobos hurtled by, a small satellite that was a smudge in the salmon-pink sky. It was hot outside, though Rick wasn't sure why. It was the first time he'd truly been out of his suit for any length of time, and he realized he'd never felt the heat and dryness before. He felt his uniform cling to him from the heat and sweat. The crowd cheered louder as he spied Ceb walking into the circle. Rick took a deep breath as he entered the circle, to a chorus of boos. The Golgoro he faced looked tough; his tribal whorls and body paint had been reapplied to contrast his red skin with the black of the body paint. He held a knife almost twenty centimeters longer than the one Rick held. Ceb also had a leonine grace as he moved through a few practice thrusts that caused Rick to feel his heart hammer against his chest. *This is going to be fun.*

Cal'Bain himself stood on a raised dais before one set of bleachers. He held his arms out, and the cheers and jeers died down. His green eyes swept over Ceb and Rick. "Before us is Wandsman Ceb Delsen. His opponent is Rick Tavish of the Space Rangers." Cal'bain waited a moment as the jeers filled the dry air. He quieted them with a wave. "This is a trial by combat. Let the Twins that watch over us settle this with blood. On my signal, begin." He raised his hands, and a bell the size of his helm hovered above his head. It was made of the same glass-like material as Rick and Ceb's knife. There was no clapper inside that Rick could see, but when he struck the air below the bell, a loud, clear peal of the bell rang out.

Rick charged forward at the signal. Ceb waited, holding the knife pointed down. Ceb brought the blade tip-up at the last moment as Rick came in for a low stab. The slash from the Golgoro would have hurt, had Rick not lunged to one side, allowing his Earthman muscle to send him ten feet from the attacker. He landed, smiling. "Well, that is one advantage," he said to himself as Ceb sneered.

His opponent snarled and rushed towards Rick, holding his arms parallel to the ground. Rick waited, holding his ground. When Ceb reached him, Rick watched as Ceb's blade dropped from one hand, and was caught by his other hand. Rick's eyes tracked the knife, and he missed the heavy punch to the side of Rick's head with Ceb's now-empty hand. Rick dropped to the ground, coughing at the dust and sand that puffed out when he landed hard. His head rang from the blow. He tried to stand, shaking his head. A shadow fell on Rick. Out of instinct, Rick rolled to one side and missed getting struck by the heavy blade's point.

"Stay still, Earthman," Ceb growled as Rick continued rolling to one side again and again as the Golgoro stabbed down repeatedly, trying to land a killing blow. As he rolled, Rick lost his own blade. Hitting the edge of the circle, a small raised wall that arrested his movement, Rick felt trapped. Ceb smirked, seeing his opponent caught. He brought down the blade, hard.

Rick's hands shot up and caught Ceb's thick, corded wrists with his own hands. The leverage wasn't there, and Ceb was stronger than Rick thought. The blade moved closer and closer to Rick's chest, moving centimeter by centimeter closer to the sigil of the Space Rangers and his heart.

Struggling against Ceb, Rick saw one slim hope open up. He had dropped his knife, but it was till close enough to grab. However, he needed both hands to keep Ceb's knife from stabbing him, as the Golgoro was pressing down with all of his weight. *What am I going to* —He stopped when the one thing that kept getting drilled into him at the Academy hit him hard. "When it comes to knife fighting, always remember one thing. *You are going to get cut.*"

Twisting his body towards his own blade, his opponent slashed down, cutting across Rick's exposed back. Yet, Rick's hand wrapped around his own blade's hilt, and he plunged it deep into the side of the wandsman. The stab was deep, and the wandsman grunted, trying to pull away from Rick. Rick's blade dragged at the man, cutting deeper, tearing open the wound. Hot, dark-red blood poured from the wound. Rick didn't let go, as Ceb struggled feebly for a moment before stopping. There was a spasm from the wandsman, then Ceb coughed blood into Rick's face and was still, dropping his head on Rick's chest.

There was a roar from the crowd, Rick realized. He blinked, and Al'Kara was there. Another psi-blade came to assist Ceb with a device like Al'Kara's, but the wandsman had succumbed to his wounds.

Rick stood up with the help of Al'Kara. He looked to Cal'Bain, whose face was a raw mask of anger. He took a long breath, trying to relax his features. When he opened his all-green eyes again, Rick felt that he and Al'Kara were doomed.

"You have proven that Ceb was the one in the wrong. Congratulations. However, you have spilled blood at a Moot. You and Al'Kara are expelled from the Moot, and Al'Kara is banished from her clan, from the Temple, and the planet."

Al'Kara sagged for a moment but took the verdict in stride. Rick wanted to say something, but he stayed quiet.

"May you always find water and shade," Al'Kara said to her uncle.

"May you find rot and ruin," her uncle whispered back.

The words stung Al'Kara; Rick could tell. She bit back an oath and helped Rick to secure his suit and then return to the skimmer. Once they left the Moot, Rick wanted to ask Al'Kara what had happened, but instead was still. He piloted the skimmer towards his rocket, feeling like he was headed home.

After an hour of standing alone at the controls, Al'Kara was next to him. Her face was damp from tears. Still, she looked at Rick and grinned.

"Why do you look happy? You were just expelled from—"

"I have free reign to do what I wish, beloved." She rested a hand on his as he piloted the craft closer to his rocket. "To journey with you, wherever you may go."

He nodded, happy to have her as a companion. The rocket itself looked none the worse for wear. With a little creative programming, he was able to edit some of the worst out of the automatic reporting. Rick mentally cataloged all of the regs he was breaking by bringing her along. All of the rules that had been a part of the Space Rangers. He didn't care. She'd helped him and saved him more than once. And he cared for her; he *wanted* her to stay with him.

"In that case," Rick said, stopping the skimmer and gesturing to the rocket, "Let's get aboard and dust off for Callisto."

TO BE CONTINUED IN *WITCH MOUNTAIN*

LON VARNADORE

WITCH MOUNTAIN

PART OF A KNOWN WORLD SERIES

WITCH MOUNTAIN

CHAPTER SIXTEEN

The sun, distant as it was too Mars, hung low in the sky when Bors spotted the marauders' first sign. He'd gone ahead to scout the edge before the dead Northern Ocean shore. The dry, shriveled chasm that once held water stretched out for Bors to see to the North. His eyes roved over a massive, dry, bed of bleached bones of ancient sea creatures with long-dead patches of seaweed gone to discolored dust. He spotted the distant trails of dust as signs of a coming force. The dust rills grew thicker and wider, speaking of the great number of the coming marauders. Once he spotted the signs of the oncoming horde, he spun to return with swiftness to those who hired him.

Unlike the *Blue Hand* merchants or a majority of those that called Mars home, Bors was able to keep pace with their wagons and scouted ahead on foot. His tribe, *The Hidden Mountain*, now lost to time, were fleet of foot. It was one of the reasons he had been hired by the *Blue Hand*. Another was for the fighting prowess he would bring to bear on marauders and cutthroats for the dyed-woad merchants. When he crested the last rise, away from the Northern Ocean basin, he saw that the horde skirmishers had gotten around him to soften the *Blue Hand*. The battle was already joined by marauding *Sharpteeth* and those of the *Blue Hand* that could wield some kind of weapon.

When he saw that it was the cannibalistic *Sharpteeth* that attacked, his rage doubled, fueled by what the villainous tribe had done to his own kith and kin. This spurred him forward. It was a losing battle from the moment Bors joined. Even his skills couldn't stop the merchant train of five wagons from being cut in half from the thirty that had hired him. The *Soul of the Mother* started to sing in his head, though he didn't wield her, not yet. He did not wish to pay *her* price if he could help it. The song still filled his eyes with a red haze, feeling his body thrum with a berserker's power. While he cut down the first few marauders with his long dagger and axe, he lost himself in the battle rage.

Coming out of the rage, shoving the cracked haft of his axe forward, Bors pushed an attacking cannibal away from him. It gave him a moment to breathe and take in the battle scene. He realized, looking over the broken remains of the caravan, *the caravan is lost. The Sharpteeth will kill everyone.* Yet, all were dead or dying, and the three *Sharpteeth* tribesman turned to focus their attacks on Bors. They laughed, licking their blades to heighten their own rage and bloodlust to overwhelm Bors.

The shove of his weapon also caused the crack along the haft to splinter more before the head of the axe dropped to the blood-caked soil. *Useless.* Bors dropped the useless axe haft with a grunt. With the axe gone, the black iron sword on his back was the only weapon left to him. He felt, more than heard, the singing of the *Soul of the Mother* in his head pitch lower, *thrumming* inside his own chest. For a heartbeat, he felt the weight of the sword lighten, desiring to come forth and taste blood. He paused, not wanting to accept more of her help. Before another moment passed, a shriek of an attacking *Sharpteeth* cannibal bearing down on him drove his instincts. His calloused hand wrapped tight around the age-worn leather of the sword hilt, pulling *Soul of the Mother* free with a single, fluid movement.

The *Soul of the Mother* weighed little in his hands. He sliced upwards, taking the top third of the first attacking cannibal's head off. *Her* song in his head was forming a full-throated dirge of death. He brought the sword blade down on the other two *Sharpteeth* that rushed towards Bors. The diagonal slash downward clove through one, with the pitted black blade stopping in the pelvis at the other, caught in the bone of the dying cannibal. Even the bone of the *Sharpteeth* clansmen didn't stop the *Soul of the Mother* for more than a moment before the blade bit through the flesh of the dead tribesman with a final flick of Bors' wrist. Drawing back his blade in a high-fighting stance by instinct, he readied himself for the next opponent. His chest heaved, hair wild and matted with sweat and blood, coating him in a fine sheen of red and pink. His eyes unfocused on anything more than the red haze before him.

A heartbeat passed before he realized he was alone with the dead. The screams and cries of the two clashing clans were gone. Bors was greeted by the silence of the dead and the slight moan of the Martian wind, blowing towards the dead Northern Ocean. Blinking in the wan Martian sunlight, he realized he stood alone, feeling his failure weigh upon him. He was the lone survivor, coated in the gore of friend and foe alike. A cold wind from the cliffs of what once was Olympus Mons rippled over his blood-caked body as the realization that he'd survived snuck in.

The sword grew heavy. Dropping the sword point to the ground, a moment later, one of Bors' knees followed to the blood-soaked red-orange sand. He looked up at the ancient bone hilt of the *Soul of the Mother,* like an idol to worship. The crossguard was a macabre collection of freely given tribesmen's' fingerbones to protect, in a cage, the small piece of *Mother,* the last bit of Olympus Mons found by a *Hidden Mountain* shaman untold years ago. It *was* Bors' idol. *An idol of death,* he thought with a grimace as the song continued in his head.

"*Soul of the Mother*, I thank you for your help, your strength," he called out, his voice hoarse and threatening to break. The song faded from his head. "I plead that you return to your home and wait for me to call forth… "

A quiver of movement started at the buried tip of the long black iron blade, traveling up the well-worn, pitted, black blade before transferring into his hands that clutched the hilt. His stomach roiled, knowing what was coming. *Not again. Not the—*

Before he could react, Bors felt the soft touch on his shoulder. He choked back an oath. Looking back over his shoulder, he saw a shawl-wrapped, hooded form standing behind him, the form fading to nothing from the waist down. The hood revealed only a matronly smile on a youthful oval face with dark eyes. Bors knew the specter well; it haunted his darker dreams and corners of his mind when he slept. *Mother*. Her dark eyes looked into him, *through* him. A translucent blue glow surrounded the form. A curl of dark hair peeked out from the shawl's hood, curling over her forehead. The hand she touched Bors with was soft, colored a baked tan of long-time exposure to sunlight. Yet, her face was pale as milk. *"What is wrong, my bearer?"* Her voice was a melodious song in Bors' heart and mind. Her lips didn't move, speaking directly into his mind.

"I am done fighting, *Mother*. There is nothing left to fight."

"You *may* need me. There is always more fighting to be had." She said this with a placid smile on her face as she touched him.

"I can survive without you for a time," he said, not looking at her. He didn't wish to anger her, but he had to sheathe her. If not, she would demand more and more of *her price*.

The grip on his shoulder grew painful. Fingernails tinged the color of old blood grew longer and sharper, digging painfully into the flesh of his bare shoulder. Her matronly face grew haggard and drawn. Her eyes were growing more intense. "You *will* have need of me, bearer!" The rictus of a loathsome grin appeared on her face. Her other hand grabbed his chin and forced Bors to look at her.

Bors quaked with fear, the pain in his shoulder blooming as her nails dug deep into his chin. Licking suddenly dry lips, he spoke in a croaking whisper, "I know, *Mother*, but, for the moment, I ask that you please rest. I will call you forth the moment I—"

The form turned from him, causing his mouth to snap closed with an audible *click*. Her shawl fell to her mid-back. Her back, as pale as her face, rippled and danced with more muscles and sinew than Bors had seen in a woman her size. Her bare skin, the color of pale milk in the weak sunlight of the sun, took on a soft glow. She didn't look back, yet her tone softened. "Very well, my bearer. Yet, I will have my payment." Her hands stretched out. Bors felt a squirm of dread through his belly, knowing what was coming next all too well. He wanted to close his eyes to the macabre scene but knew he couldn't. He *had* to be her witness.

Red mist started to ooze from the fallen bodies, the rills of mist merging into thicker and thicker streams of vermillion, swirling together towards her outstretched hands, settling on the arms and bare back of the specter of the *Soul of the Mother*. Bors felt the sword *thrum* more and more as it fed. After several heartbeats, Bors blinked and found himself alone. *Mother* was gone. The bodies of the *Sharpteeth* and *Blue Hand* merchants alike changed from freshly slain corpses to shrunken, desiccated husks that didn't look out of place in the vast stretches of the dead Northern Ocean. Bone and mummified flesh were the only remains of the *Soul of the Mother's* price. One thing had changed with the bodies. All had shifted their eyeless skulls to turn towards Bors, many with one or both arms outstretched in an inviting gesture to join them in the afterlife, begging him to join them in their eternal rest. He thought he heard a whisper, "Join us, brother. Join us with *Mother. Forever... Forever... Forever...*"

For several heartbeats, the whispers grew louder and louder. Bors waited, closing his eyes until the whispers and echoes faded to nothing. It was like his dreams of late, since returning from his adventure with Tosh and gaining the *Soul of the Mother*. A field of dead, desiccated corpses, whispering for him to join them in the embrace of *Mother.* *"All bearers share this fate..."* one whispered. *"Join us, brother..."*

Once finally alone from the voices, he turned from the dead, able to shake off the dread of the macabre ritual of his sword. He realized that it grew easier with each battle to push off the horrors of what his sword did. *As it does with killing,* he thought with a grim shake. He shrugged on the last of the surviving water harnesses, took the last of the dwindling provisions that survived the combat, and started walking away from the carnage towards the North and the vast, dead ocean that the *Blue Hand* had wished to cross. Continuing towards the polar caps and the sparse settlements, Bors hoped to find some solace there.

He didn't turn south, for he had made a pledge to his brother Tosh to travel a year and a day away from Gods' Home. Bors believed his journey North a better plan than to return so soon after setting out. He had food for a few days; with the rest of the caravan gone, it would last a week and a half. He thought he'd find someone with whom to trade and travel within a day or so. Though it was not a well-traveled route, the *Blue Hand* would not be the only ones traveling to the polar towns for trade. It buoyed his confidence and helped to shake off the horrid things he left in his wake.

CHAPTER SEVENTEEN

For three days, Bors sought some kind of respite, some succor from the badlands, without luck. Water skins were emptied and discarded. The water harness, damaged in the fight, broke completely after a day. He left the ruins of the harness's catcher on the thick, baked clay. It weighed him down, and it had no use for him. The last of the food had run out a day before the water. Still, Bors continued to walk North.

At night, the Eye of Jove burned in the sky, the twin spots of Deimos and Phobos giving a touch more illumination. Bors mused that he was near Moon Cross, the reason for the *Sharpteeth* raid on the *Blue Hand*. For his own tribe—so he'd been told by the last of his elders before they, too, perished from age and time. It was a time of reflection. He mused of where he'd come from and how here ached where he settled down. There was nothing, no scrub, no tree, no water this far from where Olympus Mons had been. *Did I make a mistake? Should I have returned to Gods' Home?* Tosh wouldn't be there. What would it matter?

Settling heavily on the red-orange clay and dirt, he looked south. At first, he sought the huge shape of Olympus Mons after seeing it in the past with Tosh. He knew that the mountain wasn't there, that he held the soul of the mountain in his hands, glancing down at the pitted and ancient-looking blade across his lap. *That was the past. Before she left.* Before the *Mother of Mountains* disappeared and came to Bors' people in the form of the black, iron sword that rested across his thighs.

It was the legend. The sword had been lost for generations. It was only through *The Master* that Bors came to possess the sword in the first place. For so long, he had only known of Olympus Mons as a myth, the legend of her as a sword. His hands rested on the cool metal as he bowed his head. "*Soul of the Mother*, what should I do?"

The image of the large mountain sprang to mind. *Mother's first form.* He counted himself blessed to have actually seen it in the strange adventure with Tosh of Deimos. Bors tried not to dwell long on the former image of the mountain. Her new form grew a little heavier across his legs. The face of Tessa and Nix, even Tosh, his brother, filled his mind instead. And how he had almost come to kill Tosh. It was a small argument after they had arrived back on Mars after *The Master* and his wife had sent them away. Tosh had gotten drunk and had spoken ill of the Hidden Mountain tribe by accident. "How could anyone worship a mountain that doesn't exist anymore?" Tosh had asked in a drunken quarrel. "It sounds like superstitious mumbo-jumbo." The besotted Tosh looked at Bors and laughed. "And to think it is now some *sword?* Come, Bors, you can't be that foolish?"

Bors knew Tosh was drunk, yet the bloodlust from the *Soul of the Mother*—one that Bors hadn't fully realized was part of her *gift*—surged in Bors, making him draw the *Soul of the Mother* on Tosh. At first, Tosh only laughed at him. As Bors raged and threatened Tosh with the *Soul of the Mother,* the drunken merchant gave a smirk while asking, "What? You are going to cut me down in cold blood, *brother?*" There was a moment of hesitation from Bors, and Tosh's smirk wavered. "Brother?" Tosh asked again.

That moment of pause caused the barbarian to shake himself from his rage. Bors dropped the point of his sword, disgusted by what he had almost done. Bors then gave Tosh a smile, laughing it off. "Never, my brother." He took a large quaff of ale to hide the look of humiliation and fear on his face. The two retired to their shared room soon after.

Bors didn't sleep much that night, the *Soul of the Mother* staying in its sheath and away from him. Yet, he couldn't be more than an arm span from it because of his connection.

The next morning, Bors suggested that the two should part for a year and a day.

"A Martian year, you mean?" Tosh asked, bemused by the idea.

"Yes," Bors said.

"So, almost two Earth years?"

"Yes." *It is better this way, Tosh.*

"Are you sure it is better this way, bearer?" Mother whispered in his ear, snapping Bors from his reverie.

"Yes!" He screamed into the wind. He looked around, seeing no manifestation appear. It was simply her voice, goading him in his head. "Tosh is stronger than you know."

"*He* is weak," the voice of Mother said. "He holds you back."

"No," Bors shouted, not believing her.

"You will die out here. You are a fool. My powers can't *help* you much longer. Your friend, *Tosh*," the words came out as more of a curse, "can't help you. Only I can help you, my bearer." The voice was plaintive. "Begin your trip back to the south, and you'll live."

Bors took a deep breath to calm his minds and emotion. "No."

"You *will* die."

For a long moment, Bors studied the dark horizon and the myriad stars and the Eye of Jove that illuminated the Martian night sky. "Maybe... but until that time comes, be silent."

"As you wish, *bearer.*" The weight of the sword doubled for a moment, crushing down on his knees, then returned to its normal weight in the blink of an eye.

Bors shook his head and continued to look over the barren ocean bed before pulling his cloak over himself, drifting off into a restless slumber.

He dreamt of the short adventures with Tosh of Deimos. Good dreams of the bizarre adventures they had. He hoped his brother was doing better, and he hoped Tessa was well.

When he dreamt of Tessa, the girl with the dragon serpent smiled at him. Then, a form loomed from Tessa's shadow. The shawled and hooded form of *Mother* appeared, driving the girl, her dragon, and Tosh away from Bors. "You'll never know their fate... This foolishness will *kill* you— and me, *my bearer.*" The shawl-wrapped form of the *Soul of the Mother* wailed and screeched louder and louder with anguish, which awakened him finally.

Brushing the sleep and dust from his eyes, Bors stood and stretched. He yawned, needing sleep, yet he knew his sword would not allow him to sleep more that night. Seeing the sun was still hours from rising, he gathered the meager possessions he retained and pressed on towards the pole of Mars.

He continued to walk until an eldritch force made him hesitate for a moment. Blinking away windswept sand from his eyes, Bors realized he'd fallen to the dead ocean floor, asleep. While walking, he'd fallen from exhaustion. Blinking open eyes gummed shut with wind and sand, he found himself staring at a stone plinth five feet in front of him. Atop it was a dark stone column of no stone native to Mars, broken by some ruinous form of destruction, giving it a shattered, ancient look. Standing, Bors felt sudden electricity in the air, hearing a faint chant echoing in his head as he crept closer to the plinth and pillar. With a grunt, he pushed himself forward past the column and found another pillar, and another, and another. Each was the remnants of a column of some kind, and none were whole. Each one had been shattered by some kind of ancient rage. Some were destroyed near the top of their seven-foot span, others near the base. No two pillars were broken in the same way or were the same length. More than one was made of some kind of crystal. The crystal ones shimmered and sparkled with a throbbing light in time to the soft chant growing louder as he explored the ruins. A whisper came to him, yet when he tried to focus on it, it slipped away into a susurrus on the wind. Then, Bors swore he heard a voice in the wind, speaking his name.

He stumbled around each of the pillars, still weak from lack of food and water. He found seven in all. Together they formed a crude circle thirty feet across. In the center was a black stone slab, ten feet square, made of something like black marble. There was something about it that felt *wrong* to Bors. Still, he moved closer. Soon, he came to the lip of the slab and studied the polished surface. It rose five feet out of the sands, yet Bors was sure there was more buried.

"Bors, we need your help," a voice said again, much clearer than before.

Bors looked around, not seeing anything. His hand went to *Mother*, yet she was cold and heavy, dragging him down. Biting back a curse, his eyes swept the circle of pillars and the stone slab. "Where are you?" He shouted, one hand pulling out his small bone dagger, not wanting to use *Mother* if he could help it. She felt more and more like a millstone upon his back.

"Come closer," the voices said. "Stand on the slab."

Bors sought the comfort of the *Soul of the Mother*. When he gripped the worn leather hilt, the sword trebled in weight, feeling like a millstone borne on his back. He released *Mother,* and the weight left him. *She doesn't want me to go?* That troubled him more, for *Mother* was not wary of much. Though he could feel the need to find out who was calling him, the thrill of some new discovery on Mars sang in his blood. For a moment, he paused. Then he gripped the edge of the marble slab, heaving himself onto the cold, slick, polished black surface.

"Bors, you are needed. Please, you have to help," the voice called out, much clearer and closer, Bors realized. A shape took form in the center of the stone slab. It was short; the head was barely up to the barbarian's thigh. The form was light yellow in color, with ears that stuck out so far, they dropped under their own weight with tufts of white fur at the tips. Otherwise, the creature was devoid of hair. The eyes were what concerned Bors. They were black. Pure, pitch black, but there was no malice or rancor in them. The creature that looked up at him from the center of the slab looked more like a whipped dog than any kind of threat. Small arms and feeble, three-fingered hands clutched a walking stick. It was naked, save a rough pair of patched and re-patched homespun shorts. The feet of the creature were splayed out in three wide toes with dark nails flecked with dirt. The body itself was hollow-chested and spindly.

"We... we need your help. Please say you will help." The voice was pleading, begging for Bors to agree.

Bors stared at the small creature. It looked terrified. He reached out, and the form drew back with fearful speed. "You have to say yes before anything can be done," the creature said. "Please..."

"What is going on?" Bors asked. He looked up and saw as he stood on the slab, a mist starting to surround the ancient area. The pulsing and the chanting grew louder and more distinct. He could see more of the figures like the one that stood before him, yet they were obscured by the pillars and by the rising fog. They looked as if they were made of shadow and no substance. "Why?"

"Will you help?" The creature on the black marble slab asked. "We have need of a hero. Are you that hero?" The hand stretched out again, quivering.

The question made Bors feel a slight smile on his lips. *A call to adventure?* His belly growled, and he hoped that wherever they were, they had food. "Yes, if you have food," Bors said, reaching forward to grasp the hand again. This time, he grasped flesh, and there was a feeling of thunder without sound that vibrated through him.

A moment later, there was a sudden rushing of wind as the chanting grew louder and louder. Bors felt his body gripped by some unseen force, stretching and crushing him. The air exploded from his lungs as it was yanked out by force. He collapsed to the ground, shaking and gasping for breath like a landed fish. Finally, he felt himself lifted off the black slab of marble an arm's length, unable to do more than feel his stomach flip-flop inside him before crashing down upon the black, very solid slab of marble; stunned by the violent forces for a heartbeat.

He stood, *Mother* clearing his scabbard before he realized that she weighed less than a feather. *Mother, what is—*

"You said you would help us," the creature that had spoken said again, though this time, his words were more distinct, clearer. Bors turned to find that the creature in the flesh replaced the image of the creature. The creatures cowered, holding hands up to shield their wrinkled, shriveled faces. He was no longer surrounded by the plinths of stone in the dry sands of Mars. Natural cavern walls surrounded him, with yellow stone columns that looked to be of worked stone. There were still seven pillars. Each of them now looked more intact than the ones he had seen moments before.

"What happened?" Bors shouted, realizing then that his head was ringing, and he could not hear anything. He felt something pulling him down more. *Mother*'s weight had trebled, pulling him down. He grunted, dug his heels in, and kept himself standing.

"You agreed to help us on Callisto. You have been brought to our aide," the creature said.

"Show me!" Bors growled.

The leader pointed towards a large cavern entrance. The other creatures that surrounded the marble square pulled back from Bors' bellow and retreated more as he stepped down onto a stone path filled in with hard-packed dirt.

Bors looked around, stunned to see that the sky that greeted him was strange and foreign. No longer were the two bright forms of the Twins, Deimos and Phobos, looming in the sky. Instead, a large red blob of a dark red sun took up the majority of his view. Though, as he swept his gaze from the dark red sun, he could see the ragged edge of black of the night of the horizon. Along the surface of the dark red sun, he saw what looked like molten whorls and boiling swirls of moving liquid. "That looks like the Eye of Jove, yet closer?"

"It *is* the Eye. You are on Callisto now, hero," the creature said, extending a shaky clawed hand. "I am Ghurd."

Bors tested the air, and there was a wet slap that hit him when he left the cave. And, it was filled with sweet scents from the overabundance of vegetation he saw on the green world. It was strange and disorienting for a moment, though it was not the first time Bors had been off-world. Usually, it was done with Gates; however, Bors grasped what had happened and looked forward to the new adventures that would take place on this world.

Bors took a long breath and thought he heard the cackle of *Mother* in the back of his head. And then the words, "I told you so," rang in his head before going silent again.

At least she does not weigh me down anymore. Bors patted *Moth-*

er's pommel while looking around. "What do you need help with?" Bors asked. He knew his sword might not have wanted him here, but he was here now. She would still have her payment bounty and help him with her strength.

"There is a witch in the mountains, north of here. She appeared months ago. She dominates more and more of my clan. We are too scared to flee and too weak to fight. This is our *homeland*. We can't escape her mental domination. We need you to kill her. Once that has happened, we will be free of her control."

Bors nodded without hesitation. He'd done this kind of work many times, regardless of where he was. "I shall do as you ask. It is an easy task to kill a witch."

The Callistians surrounded him, letting out whoops and odd hoots of joy after he made his pronouncement.

"What is this place?" Bors asked, looking over the decrepit cavern, which he realized was the entrance to some ancient temple.

"A place to come and beseech help from the gods," Ghurd said. "It had lain dormant for generations, forgotten by most after the Purge of Salkardin. It was our one last hope to find someone to help us fight the witch."

"And I was the one it brought?" Bors asked, looking at the assembled creatures and their leader.

"Yes, you will help us. You are the hero who comes to us, in different forms, of course, to help the Callistians, as the legend says," Ghurd said. "Soon, you will find your partner, and the pair of you will kill the witch."

Bors looked at Ghurd with a raised eyebrow. "What partner?" *Do they mean Tosh?*

"The hero will journey here alone, yet he will find his partner on the way," Ghurd said, intoning it as if it were from some ancient legend.

Bors cocked an eye. *Could Tosh come to this planet? Would we work together again?* The idea made him smirk. He would do much to have a friendly face with him. Though Tosh was more adept at talking than fighting, Bors trusted that his brother would help if he were here.

For a price, so it is good he is not here, or Ghurd would have to give something before Tosh agreed. I'd never hear the end of it. It was the one quality of Tosh that Bors thought was strange. Yes, Bors expected payment. Yet, to kill a witch was an honorable thing for the *Hidden Mountain.*

As his eyes roved the horizon, Bors noticed a curious light that appeared right under the light of the Eye. It flickered from red to yellow, to green, and back. "What is that?" Bors asked, pointing towards the edge of the horizon.

"That is where you must go," Ghurd said. "It is there that you will find Witch Mountain, where the vile sorceress who has enslaved our brethren resides. Follow that light, hero, and you will find your quarry."

CHAPTER EIGHTEEN

After a brief respite for water and to refill the water harness that he still carried and to take a few small packets of food that Ghurd and his people thrust towards him, he set off to follow the light they had pointed out. Bors found the planet to have a strange verdant and lush beauty. He had not been to Callisto, and seeing the primal beauty of the planet, he enjoyed it.

Yet, there were pitfalls as well. A peculiar thing was the red flowers that grew rampant in patches and bunches of ten to fifteen. The stalks looked much like grass, but thicker and topped with a blood-red bloom with an eye-like stamen in the center. What was worse was the eldritch way they followed Bors as he moved by them. On more than one occasion, he plucked one. The "eye" of the flower burst from the center of the flower, to slowly drift to the ground, then burrow itself in the soft loam. On a whim, Bors grabbed at one when he saw it burst out, only to have it *pop* in his hand, leaving his palm stinging for the majority of the day.

There were also the panther-like creatures that stalked through the underbrush. Bors heard the roaring cry as a kind of twilight fell on the first day. The roar caused his blood to surge with the desire to fight or flee. He set his lips in a smirk, knowing what he would do. When the black lion-like creature erupted from the underbrush, Bors was partially ready. He had been expecting the creature to leap out from a small copse of trees to his left, but it leaped out from seemingly nowhere close by. Bors let out a startled grunt as the thing fastened its teeth on his arm, bowling over the large barbarian. When he slammed to the ground, he could not pull *Mother* from the baldric in time. His free hand went to his belt, pulling the smaller dagger from his hip and slamming it repeatedly into the throat and neck of the creature. At first, his thrusts were, once again, against a phantom creature that was not where he thought.

"Let the pain guide you, bearer," the voice of *Mother* whispered in his head.

He closed his eyes without thinking and let the gnawing pain in his left arm guide his strikes. Moments later, he was able to dispatch the panther-like creature. He bound the wound as he looked down at the carcass of the creature and whispered a quick prayer to the *Soul of the Mother* before turning to butcher the creature for meat.

He was thankful for it since the Callistians provided him with fruit and fish, which was good, but the fish was small, and Bors had finished it in the first meal after he had set out. The panther-like creature's meat would help, he mused while cooking large chunks of it. He did wish he had time to salt or cure more of the meat properly, but there was not much light or heat from the Eye of Jove, and he wasn't sure how long sun-curing the meat would take.

On the third day, Bors was in a small vale with a stream running along the center and the eye-like stalks of flowers that continued to stare at him. The flowers unnerved Bors, as though they watched and followed him. It was unnerving, and the stinging in his hand waxed and waned if he moved closer to the different patches of flowers. He then caught sight of something shining on the slight path he found himself following and forgot about the flowers for the moment.

It was the body of a prostrate, clothed human, lying on their stomach, unmoving.

Bors cocked an eyebrow as he looked at the unconscious human. The man—at least Bors thought it was a man—was clothed in something that was red and gold. It looked shiny and form-fitting. The shininess had been what drew Bors' eye. The man had something gripped in one hand that gave Bors pause. It took a moment before Bors realized it was much like the ray gun Tosh had used in their travels, except this one looked thicker and not as streamlined. For a moment, he missed his brother Tosh again.

Bors wasn't sure what to do with the unconscious man. He didn't look hurt, only unconscious. Bors moved to the body, going to one knee to poke at the unconscious man with a thick finger, and the other man groaned in a soft, sleepy way.

Bors reached out to shake the man's shoulder. The red-and-gold clothed man jerked up and away in a burst of sudden energy. He threw himself backward, seeing Bors, causing the man to hit the soft dirt and grass with a sudden *thump* on his rump. He brought the ray gun up to bear on Bors as he fell. Bors waited, holding his hands outward to show no weapons in his hands. The man stopped, looking around confused. "Where... where am I? Where's Al'Kara?" He turned to look at Bors squarely. "What have you done with Al'Kara?" The ray gun was now held more menacingly towards Bors. "Where is she?"

The words were strange in Bors' ears. It was like the "civilized" land's Trade Tongue, yet something sounded off. The words had a strange inflection to them. "You are on a planet of Jove's Eye," Bors said, pointing towards the large dark ember that was the Eye of Jove above them.

The man's hand went to his neck. "Wait! My helmet's gone. Damn, my suit is gone! How? What is— How can I breathe so easily?" He gave a look up, then around, with more agitation. His free hand went to his suit, patting around trying to find something. The man gave Bors another look, and he lowered the weapon. "I am sorry for that, training and all. Do you know how I got here?"

Bors shrugged. "I don't know. Are you hurt?"

"No, only confused," the man said, looking around. Confusion and fear knitted his brow over his dark brown eyes. He looked to be a head shorter than Bors, though in good health. A moment later, the man finger-raked his dark brown hair and lowered his weapon. "Protocol never covered this, though I can hope the suit is still in the ship itself, wherever *it* is." He gave Bors a long, appraising look and then holstered his weapon. "I wish I had my suit. I'd be able to figure out more with its instruments." He then looked at Bors and gave him a smile. "Which moon of Jove?"

"You are an odd one," Bors said with a small grin. He then offered the odd man his hand up.

"Why do you say that?" The man asked, taking the offered hand. Once he stood, he dusted himself off. He gave Bors a smile. "You a native to this moon?"

Nodding at the ray gun, Bors smiled. "You put your weapon away even though you don't know who I am. And, no. I am from Mars."

"If you were going to attack, you'd have attacked when I was unconscious. Or taken advantage of me while I was unconscious, and I'd never have woken up. I think I'm safe with you." The man gave Bors another smirk. "I just left there with Al'Kara." His smile turned to a frown. "We need to find her."

"We will find your mate."

"She is not my... She is a *friend*."

Bors rolled his eyes. He didn't understand why the "civilized" people had such hang-ups about bedmates or life mates. "Of course. You are honorable." He saw that the man didn't understand Bors' words. "Have I confused you, man?"

"You say I am honorable because I didn't shoot you? That sounds like good manners," the man said with a shrug. "Plus, not my style to shoot without knowing why I am shooting. What's your name?"

"Bors, of the *Hidden Mountain*."

"This doesn't look like the Tharsis Plains," the man said, looking around with a wry grin.

"It's not, we are on the dark planet of Callisto, watched over by Jove personally, but I have given you my name," Bors said, waiting for the man to name himself.

"I'm Rick Tavish, Space Ranger," Rick said, a hand extending towards Bors. "A pleasure, Bors."

Bors cocked his head to the side. "I have never heard of the *Space Rangers*. Where does that tribe reside?" Bors clasped Rick's hand and squeezed the thick, eldritch, metal gauntlet on his wrist.

Rick gave a small laugh. "I suppose the Rangers are 'my tribe,' but if you tell that to the commander, she'll rip you a new one. Verbally, of course." He started to tap away at a small device on his wrist. "That is strange. I can't get any reading of my ship. Or of any Ranger buoys." He started to push more buttons. "This makes no sense. I wonder what... damn, Al'Kara." He shook his head. "She needs to be our top priority. Have you seen anyone else?"

"No," Bors said. "We can look."

"I only hope Al'Kara is alive and close by," Rick said as he started to move away from Bors.

"What are Ranger buoys?" Bors asked.

"Satellites in space that help communications to the rest of the Consortium. Wait, I'm getting a very, very weak signal coming from space... and one from the mountains to the north of us."

Both looked in the direction of the low series of hills and then the one lone spire of rock that was Bors' destination under the light of Jove's Eye. He had made a little progress, he realized, for he saw the top of the mountain was rounded and had an odd design his eyes couldn't discern at first. The name "Consortium" made no sense to Bors. Yet, Rick already looked confused, and though he was trying to stay calm, the Space Ranger looked like he didn't want to be asked any more questions until they found his mate. Instead, Bors nodded, "That mountain is my destination as well."

"Something is there," Rick said.

Bors nodded. "Then your path and mine are joined, Rick Tavish of the Space Rangers. I've been tasked to seek the Witch of the Mountain and slay her." Bors tapped the thick longsword on his back, his hand caressing the pommel for a long moment. The face of the dark-eyed *Mother* came to him with a blood-soaked smile. He pushed the thoughts away. *At least she wished bloodshed.* He hoped that Tosh was well.

"Did I lose you, Bors?" Rick asked, snapping his fingers in front of Bors' face. "You seemed to have gone off and away for a moment."

"Old thoughts," Bors said with a smirk. "Shall we continue?" He moved forward, eager to reach the mountain and complete his task before *Mother* grew more impatient.

"I could use some water," Rick said, looking at the waterskin on Bors' hip. "If that isn't too much—"

Before he could finish, Bors pulled the skin free from his belt and tossed it to Rick. "You have proven honorable, and if you wish for a water pact, then so be it." *Let's see if this 'civilized man' knows what I ask for.*

"That is when we both drink and make the bond of sharing water and life?" Rick asked. Bors felt a small shock as Rick continued. "Learned about the basics in training. Needed it on Mars... well, the Mars of my time. Al'Kara showed me the ritual and was my first... *water friend* is I think what you call them?"

"Who is this woman you speak of? You've said her name several times. Is she your betrothed?"

Rick's face flushed from Bors' question. "No, she's a *friend* who... She's a little shorter than me, dark and ruddy skin, black hair."

There was a look in Rick's eyes that Bors recognized as Rick spoke of this Al'Kara. *He's in love with her.* A disturbing thought came to Bors. "How long were you unconscious, Rick Tavish?"

"I've no way of knowing," Rick said with a shrug. "But the explosion on entry to Callisto couldn't have been that long ago. Maybe half a day." He then looked around. "Though none of this looks familiar. My ship should be close." He then checked his wrist. "Yet, I'm not getting any readings from it."

Bors let out a pent-up breath. *Good. Perhaps this Al'kara is also a captive of this witch.*

"She's also a Golgoro woman of Mars. Maybe you—"

"The Golgoro? They are a myth of Mars," Bors said with a chuckle.

Rick gave Bors a small smile. "I assure you, *She* is no myth. What about the Green Martians?"

Bors looked at Rick as though he was simple. "Those are mostly stories to frighten children. The Golgoro never existed. The *Hazak* are monsters, and they've been wiped out." Saying the name caused a shiver to run down Bors' spine. *He's crazy.* Still, he did remind himself that he had seen the *Hazak* and dealt with them with Tosh. He pushed the thought aside. *They don't live anymore. This man must be touched in the head.* And, then, another thought came to him. *Do you wish to share a water pact with him?*

Rick rubbed at his chin. "There is more to this than you would think, but please, we should have a water pact."

Bors was still surprised by Rick's words. He felt a small swell of pride and felt more honor for this man. "Yes, you're right. You know how to begin?"

"Mars *was* my first assignment, so yes," Rick said. "And, Al'kara helped." There was a small, longing look he gave to the air before shaking it off. Rick paused, holding the skin with a slight frown.

"Is something wrong?" Bors asked.

"Thinking of Al'Kara. She was with me when we entered Callisto's atmosphere. Everything after that is hazy. I can only hope she is close by."

"After the pact, we can look for her," Bors said. He didn't know why, yet he felt he *had* to have a water pact with Rick of the Space Rangers before they could continue forward. He didn't think it was *Mother* who whispered it. Something inside him urged Rick silently to start the pact ceremony. He let out a small sigh when Rick started.

Rick smiled. "I am sure she would be very angry if she thought she couldn't handle herself, but I'd appreciate the help, Bors." He then took a long sip of the water. "May we share water, sweat, and food."

Bors took the offered waterskin and took a long pull of the water. "And may we bond over blood and salt as well." He held the skin out to Rick, who took it with a nod.

"So mote it be," Rick said and took another drink.

He knows the full ceremony. He's a very strange one. But, a good man. I am glad I found him.

"Tell me more of this mission," Rick asked. "Must you kill this witch?"

Bors saw the flash of concern. "She invaded Callisto, taking a tribe of the Callistian people as her thralls. Making them do things they'd never do using sorcery to ensnare their minds. Such things cannot be done. Killing her will be for the best."

Rick looked stricken for a moment. "Are you unwell, friend Rick?" Bors asked.

"No," he said after a long pause, "Taken by their plight is all."

Bors didn't like how Rick spoke. There was something untrue in Rick's words. Something didn't *feel* right. They had pacted, and there was something on Rick's mind, yet he would not share. Bors ignored it and continued with his story as they continued to look around the small vale. Rick's color returned as Bors spoke. And Bors was glad to have a traveling companion again.

"I think that your *friend* Al'Kara is not here, Rick Tavish." Bors said after an hour of fruitless searching.

Crestfallen, Rick nodded in agreement. "Perhaps we will find her on the way to this Witch Mountain."

Bors nodded, turned, and started to move back towards his goal. It felt good to have someone to travel with, and then the words of Ghurd came back to him about "finding his companion on the road to the Mountain." Bors knew that he was in good company.

The two found themselves following a meandering, green-tinged river. Rick looked at it with a wary eye, as did Bors. The banks of the river were steep, and as they moved from the valley floor out, the river dropped more and more. Bors didn't like having the cliff to his right, but it was the only way to navigate through the thick jungle. Rick voiced his own concern.

As Rick spoke, Bors took a sniff of the air, detecting something rank and *wrong.* He stiffened, throwing a hand back to stop Rick. "Be wary, Rick, there is something—"

Before he finished, there was a scream, an inhuman shrill that echoed through the woods around them. Thirty of the yellow, wizened Callistians bore down on them. Short spears, daggers, razor-sharp claws, and even *Sharpteeth* were brought to bear on the pair. Bors unleashed *Soul of the Mother,* cutting down three of them in a single, wide cutting arc. He was about to cut down another pair when a bolt of green shot from Rick's ray gun with a *zing* to strike at Bors' intended target.

Bors turned to see that the Space Ranger had pulled a knife with a rounded tip from his boot, using it to defend himself against the short spears that three of the little creatures used to attack at him. Bors roared, charging heedlessly towards his companion. The barbarian took two spear thrusts in the back for his recklessness. The song of *Soul of the Mother* echoed in his ears, and his stamina allowed him to ignore the jabs. The creatures were small, yet their weapons left burning wounds in Bors' flesh. The stinging felt like gentle touches in the depths of Bors' fury. Blood trickled down his back. He also felt the *Soul of the Mother* starting to sing her song of bloodlust pouring into his head and body. It brought a new zeal to his fighting. Bors felt his mouth open, starting to sing the song in a deep baritone.

Bors cut down two more creatures while moving closer to Rick. Without a word, Rick spun to one side, pressing his back to Bors. The two focused on fending off the remains of the creatures. The waves attacked the pair, ending with more and more bodies piled before the two. A gang of six pressed in close for a moment, their spears punching through the lines of defense, licking out like serpents to taste the blood of the two men. Then there was a shrill whistle, and they backed off three paces.

"What the—"

Before Rick finished, sharp, stone-tipped spears rained down on them. Most of the missiles missed or scratched their extremities. Neither of them took more than minimal damage. Bors let out an inhuman howl, charging forward towards the jungle. He felt Rick moving alongside, his ray gun firing, again and again, *zing zing zing* flashes of bright green streaking towards the pairs' unseen enemies. The Callistians were no match for the pair; they'd hoped that sheer numbers would be enough. It was not.

Together, Bors and Rick dispatched their attackers with ease. Bors felt his flagging strength and weakness slowing his reactions to a crawl once the last of the Callistians was cut down. Rick shook his head. "Nasty little beasts. Glad this uniform has a Kevlar base, or I'd have been hurt worse. How did you—"

Bors heard something in the underbrush and turned, pushing himself in front of Rick as the largest Callistian that Bors had ever seen emerged from the forest, some strange device in hand. It fired at Rick, sending a bolt the size of an infant's arm hurtling towards the Ranger. Bors pushed himself in front of his water brother, taking the large bolt through the chest. He pitched backward, stumbling, trying to grab something. Bors felt his sandaled feet come out from under him. He slipped in the mud, his bulky body slamming backward down the embankment the two had avoided and splashed into the river. And then — unconsciousness.

CHAPTER NINETEEN

Without thinking, Rick swallowed a deep breath while plunging into the river after his unconscious friend, Bors. The shock of the ice-cold water threatened to rip the air from Rick's lungs. It took every ounce of will to not scream in pain and shock. Mere moments later, his hands started growing numb from the shocking cold. Rick started swimming after Bors. His friend was caught in the current, drifting away from him. Pushing the pain aside, Rick focused on reaching Bors as fast as possible. The barbarian had taken a bolt to the chest to save Rick and would drown if Rick didn't reach him in time. *Or succumb to the frigid water. Have to get to him quick and warm him up somehow,* Rick thought. Part of his mind tried to find ways to help warm him before he shunted it away. *One problem at a time!*

Rick wasn't the best swimmer, and the swift current pulling the hulking form of Bors didn't help. The one good thing was the current pulled Rick along as well as Bors in the same direction. Digging deep inside, Rick forced himself to swim faster. *He's a friend. No matter what, save him.* He closed the gap, though his lungs were starting to burn with the need for air. *Bors will be worse. If only I had my suit.*

Rick was close enough to reach out, and he tried to grasp the unconscious man's limp arm. Bors slipped from Rick's grip. Thanks to an eddy, Rick was pulled rapidly away from Bors. His lungs burned for air, and finally, he kicked himself to the surface of the river, gasping for the sweet, moist air that was waiting for him. He sucked in and out several breaths to help expand his lungs for a few more precious seconds of air before slipping underwater and kicking towards the barbarian again. With renewed vigor, the space ranger forced his cold-stiffened muscles towards the form of his friend and reached out to snag Bors' wrist! Gripping the slippery, yet corded forearm as best he could, Rick pulled hard upward. Buoyed by the water, Bors and Rick breached the water. Even Bors, in his half-conscious state, coughed out water and started to cough and suck in great gulps of air. As the barbarian gasped, he did not flail. Bors also felt a bit warmer already against Rick's thin uniform.

Safe for a moment, Rick tucked an arm under Bors' shoulder and head to keep him from slipping back into the water. "Hold on, big guy, we'll get—"

A low rumbling sound that Rick hadn't picked up at first started to build up louder and louder in the background. Rick finally noticed. At first, he thought it was only the roaring of the blood in his ears. Then, he realized the current was starting to pick up, sweeping Bors and Rick faster downriver. *Not good,* Rick realized what was going on a heartbeat before the pair slipped into a section of rapids. While in a desperate bid to keep Bors' head above water, the pair were smashed and spun in head-wrenching circles in the current. Rick tried to keep his own head from being slammed under or slammed into rocks that threatened to drive the wind from him. Barely keeping ahold of the barbarian, the two exited the rapids. For a moment, Rick felt some relief. Rick then spotted the building up of foam in the river ahead, the roar growing louder and louder still. Rick saw the beginnings of an edge to the water appear. A longer drop approached with great speed, Rick realized.

The roar was deafening.

Rick took a gulp of air. *Al'Kara, I hope you're safe.* It was Rick's last conscious thought before he and Bors plunged into the cataract of water, tumbling down through the air towards the rocks and churning water thirty meters below.

CHAPTER TWENTY

"Al'Kara, I need your help again," La'Haja called from another chamber.

"Of course, cousin," Al'Kara said as she swayed into the main laboratory chamber towards La'Haja and the Callistian. The smell was strong with antiseptic. A handful of the Callistian-altered guards stood watching or being forced to help feed and watch their smaller brethren from making too much noise from the rows of cages along the far wall. Al'Kara did detect a sharp scent of unwashed bodies that the antiseptic smell didn't fully mask. She watched as her arrival caused a stirring of agitation in the caged Callistians; several of the cage doors had to be smacked by the guards with thick palms or clubs. She made a note to inform La'Haja of it.

Al'Kara took a moment to take in the changes in the two types of Callistians: the guardian creatures and those in the cages. Broader of the shoulder, close to a meter-and-a-half tall, with thicker, sharper fangs and teeth in their jaws, some held simple clubs and jagged spears, but they were inexperienced in their use. They had been altered into these large, brutish versions to be used as guards, though they were stupid in the ways of war and still tended to attack things with their hands more than with their crude weapons.

Some were servants that La'Haja had made from the captive Callistians—like the one who had been strapped to the surgical table. Al'Kara knew she was being used by her cousin. She wasn't stupid—without Al'Kara's Mind Blade powers, La'Haja's magic would be useless. Yet the spell La'Haja had to put on her to break the strange bond with the Space Ranger, Rick Tavish, was needed. When La'Haja found them, her cousin had helped free her, and the spell kept Al'Kara free and safe. It was the only way to help her cousin.

Al'Kara *had* to help La'Haja find the cure for the Long Death, the Golgoro-only disease. It was the only way to allow the Golgoro to survive the oncoming apocalypse. It was the *only way*, La'Haja had said to Al'Kara since she'd arrived. *The only way,* the words singing in her head again and again. For a moment, the briefest flash of worry came to Al'Kara about the space ranger, Rick. It was driven from her mind, for she knew he was the enemy of La'Haja and would do anything to stop her from finding a cure for the *long death* of Al'Kara and La'Haja's people, the Golgoro.

"Are you ready?" La'Haja asked from behind a mask made of raw, grey silk. Al'Kara mentally ensnared a surgical robe and face mask of grey silk waiting on a peg at the entrance. Her mind manipulated the strings to make them both tight to her skin without contaminating the protective coverings with her own body oils. "I am ready," Al'Kara said, nodding and stepping closer to La'Haja's left side.

"Good," La'Haja said. She gestured for one of the servants to bring forth a large syringe and large-bore needle. The syringe was made of glinting green glass and polished brass, giving the tool a small degree of style. *La'Haja would want something pretty even* here, Al'Kara thought while picking it up with her mind. The amber fluid in the vial sloshed with the movement of La'Haja's latest formula combination to stave off the *long death*. It was what all of the seers of Mars had called the coming plague. The Golgoro, or what Rick and his people called the Martians, would succumb to a massive extinction-level disease by the end of the *Decade of Brass* if no one did anything. She had seen it, and yet none of the Golgoro Elders would lift a finger to stop it.

"This had better work," La'Haja said. "It must be administered—"

Al'Kara cut off her cousin. "I *was* paying attention when you told me this earlier, cousin," she said, the syringe hanging a scant half-inch from the small, yellow-skinned Callistian's jugular. It bulged out thanks to the restraints and the thrashing of the simian-like being. "I will wait until *you* finish the incantations over this creature. Please, begin."

La'Haja cast a sidelong look at her cousin, then started to intone the venerable language of Mars, flowing from one complex ancient word to the next in a melodic voice. Meanwhile, her hands hovered over the Callistian's heart. La'Haja's hands started to glow a soft wan green, *still a touch more to sickly yellowish-green that I'd like,* Al'Kara thought with a wince. Though uncomfortable with the darker, sinister color of her cousin's magic, Al'Kara *knew*. It couldn't be avoided. *Not with the long death so close.* Last time Al'Kara had been on Mars, she'd glimpsed others with the beginning of the wasting disease and had been happy to flee with Rick off Golor—*Mars. Why would I flee with him if he's my enemy?* She pushed the horrid images and questions aside, choosing to focus on the task at hand.

With the last of La'Haja's words intoned, Al'Kara's mind shoved the large-bore needle into the jugular vein of the small creature. It let out a pathetic cry as the needle sank into the thick vein. A wail tore from the creature's thrashing form as the amber fluid was injected with a mental push of the syringe. Once finished, the empty syringe was plucked free to hover over the hole made. The torn flesh and vein looked as though it was already healing itself. Al'Kara hadn't pulled the needle away fast enough, for the flesh crept over the needle, pulling it back into the growing puckered scar of the Callistian's jugular.

La'Haja and Al'Kara, sensing that the creature was healing his wounds fast, felt a growing sense of hope. They looked into each other's eyes and saw the same look of hope. Al'Kara could see hope in La'Haja's dark violet eyes, reflecting Al'Kara's own hope. *Maybe... maybe this time...*

Before they could finish their thought, the creature spasmed with a noiseless shriek, cracking open its jaws beyond the breaking point, and then the creature found its voice, and the wail of agony clawed at

Al'Kara's ears. It strained and jerked hard against the restraints. Al'Kara reached out, to try and untether them, seeing the way the flesh of the test subject abraded itself—and then started to re-grow the flesh *over* the straps. La'Haja slapped at her hand. Jerking her hand back, for a brief instant, Al'Kara felt the flare of her psi-blade solidify in her hand. *No... there is only peace. A blade can only be used with stillness of mind.* She banished the blade, not wanting to see what color it could have been.

The pair watched. Al'Kara felt sympathy and a touch of empathic pain for the creature while it writhed, the scream starting to grow weaker. The un-altered Callistians in their cages were silent for a moment as the scream stopped, yet the agony still twisted the test subject's face. Then, the cages erupted in a cacophony of screeches and banging, howls of rage and thirst for revenge.

The subject's skin and flesh continued to grow over the straps, regenerating faster and faster, unable to stop itself from halting the healing process. After five minutes, the mass of growing muscle and flesh was as large as the operating table itself. La'Haja dropped her hand, and an angry sigh escaped her lips.

Al'Kara let out a sigh and raised her right hand to the pulsating flesh blob that was the creature. Summoning her mind-blade with the stillness needed, her projected psi-blade emerged as a thin stiletto rising from her middle finger. She shoved her hand into the growing mound of flesh, approximately where the brain stem was located. She felt the resistance against the blade, and the thing continued to grow from a heartbeat. She moved her hand lower, mentally widening the blade that emerged from her left hand, slicing through the creature's chest, cutting through and around the heart to stop it from growing. For several heartbeats, the thing continued to grow. Al'Kara growled, a flicker of red curling along the pale blue psi-blade, widening the blade more and eviscerating the heart tissue. After a spastic shudder of breath from the thing, it stopped moving and died.

"That was a dismal failure," La'Haja said, ripping her mask off with her hands.

"A pity. It looked like it was working," Al'Kara said, dismissing the blade. She clenched her hands to keep them from trembling, working her mask's ties with her mind to give it something else to focus on instead of dwelling on the color of the blade.

"Destroy it, get another one. We *have* to find a cure."

"Of course, cousin," Al'Kara said. With a few deft strokes, she carved the thing up and was able to have the guards tow the bloody sections away to be disposed of.

CHAPTER TWENTY-ONE

B ors found himself alone standing on the red-orange sands of Mars, bloody and dead tribesmen around him as he had found them years ago. He'd returned with money and weapons for his tribe fighting as a mercenary and returned to death. Amongst the corpses were the four-armed green Martians. It was a large party, but the Hidden Mountain Tribe had cut down many of their numbers as well. He remembered it was then that he found his tribe's treasure, the one thing they were to guard forever, the *Soul of the Mother* had been taken. Yet Bors knew that it hung on his back even as he stood there.

A figure shimmered into view. At first, Bors gripped his new steel sword and took a stance, though something felt wrong. His chest hurt. His body was wracked by a coughing fit. He then felt dizzy as the reality hit him. He remembered the large bolt taking him in the chest and pitching him into the river. He remembered the bone-jarring cold that sapped his strength. The image of his friend, Rick, taking him up to try and help Bors' half-drowned body. Then, falling through the air and the pain of slamming into the water again and blackness. He knew the form before him, the dark, shawl-wrapped form of *Mother*.

"Do you know why you are here?" Mother asked in her sepulchral voice.

"I am dying, and you are showing me my ancestors?"

The youthful-looking chin and mouth quirked into a twisted half-smile. "Something along those lines. *But* I can make you even *stronger*, my bearer. I can give you more of my strength. All you need do is ask."

"No," Bors said, looking away from her. "I will not lose more of myself to you."

"Lose *what*?" Mother asked with a rasping, husky laugh. "You are the last of your tribe. You are alone."

"I have friends! Tosh of House du'Val. Rick of the Space—"

"They would turn their backs on you if they knew what a murderer you were," Mother said, her voice a whisper in his ear.

"No," Bors said, closing his eyes. He knew she would try more.

And she did…

Bors was suddenly a child of ten, watching an even earlier raid as the last of the Tribe of the Hidden Mountain fought a bloody skirmish with the Green Martians. Even at a young age, he tried to help but was knocked aside as an elder came to his aide to take a mortal wound meant for Bors. The skirmishing group was slaughtered, Bors was trapped under the dead body of his mentor. He tried to move the body and couldn't. Bors heard the growling, hissing laugh of a Green Martian as it crawled towards his trapped form. Murder was in the severely injured Martian's eyes. It raised up on its smaller, lower hands, with a dagger in a trembling overhead grasp. The Martian mumbled something in its language, sputtered, and coughed up a dark ichor. Succumbing to its wounds, the Green Martian simply dropped, landing atop the prone form of the Hidden Tribe's elder Bors was trapped beneath.

"Without me, you are *nothing*," Mother hissed as the creature moved closer and closer. "You are weak and worthless. I should *never* have saved you then."

Bors shook his head, knowing what the *Soul of the Mother* was trying to do. He let out a roar, "Then I am *nothing*!"

CHAPTER TWENTY-TWO

Bors sat up from the rock floor, screaming he was nothing. Rick turned and looked at him. The fever was getting worse. Bors flailed around, pinning Rick with a stare, and said, "I am nothing. I am nothing. I am nothing," before he dropped back to the stone floor of the cave, unconscious. Though, he had somehow still kept ahold of the sword. Rick was truly amazed by that.

Rick moved over to check Bors, finding him cold to the touch. The spill over the falls had knocked loose the bolt. That was the *only* plus. That and the water being ice cold had helped staunch the worst of the wound, but it had left the big man trembling with a hacking cough. The fire Rick had built in the small overhang cavern wasn't warming him enough and the cough troubled Rick. He didn't know what to do. His survival training had been a little lacking over this since he usually had his suit to help him recover or had his kit and his ship. All he had now was his Tellic ray gun, which wouldn't help in the least.

Sitting up, he rested his forehead on his knees. He was unsure. Nothing in his lessons helped. He'd done his best with the limited medical knowledge given to him, yet it wasn't enough. His friend was going to die. He didn't know what else to do. Resting his head on his knees, he whispered, "Al'Kara, I *need* you. Where are you?"

He didn't expect any kind of answer, and then— *Rick, beloved, is that you?*

"Al'Kara?" Rick shouted out in his mind, his head snapping up, half-expecting to see her there. "Are you—"

Al'Kara's mental words gave Rick comfort. "I'm glad you are close, my love. When are you coming to help?" There was something in her question that felt cut off, yet Rick pushed the thought aside.

"Help with what?" Rick asked out loud.

The semi-transparent form of Al'Kara appeared before him. Her green skin was muted by the wan light of the campfire. Her form was cut off about her waist. "My cousin. She needs help with the little Callistians." Al'Kara said mentally with a hint of a laugh. "I told you before. Remember?"

Rick felt his face contort in rage. "Your cousin is the *witch*, isn't she?" He asked out loud. "The one causing all of this hardship and twisting of the poor natives of this world?"

"No more than I am, Rick. *Please*, no need to use such archaic terms." Rick could *feel* Al'Kara's eyes roll with her mental words.

"Al'Kara, Bors needs your *help*," Rick said, trying to change the subject. He didn't have time to argue with Bors dying. "Please... *I need* your help."

"He'll get help, and so will you. You are *so* close, beloved. You are so close to help."

Rick started, "Where—"

"I'm in a nearby village. Bring your friend. He feels feverish," her form said telepathically while she stood closer to Bors. "However, you should give him something to reduce the fever, so he has a chance to survive until I can tend to him."

She looked directly at Rick, deeply. He felt images coming through of some kind of tree. The name that came to his mind was willow, yet it didn't look anything like one. *It is the same thing—it looks different here on Callisto. The bark of this tree will help reduce the fever,* Al'Kara mentally said.

Thank you, Al'Kara, Rick thought to the Golgoro as she faded. He realized when he stepped from the overhanging shelf that he was close to a small copse of them, and he was thankful. He did not think about Al'Kara as he sought the small copse of trees, or when he took his boot knife to scrape off a section of bark and set about his task. He threw himself into his work, preparing the bark as best he could—this he *could* do. There was a small bit of memory that Al'Kara had imparted to him. It had to do with crushing up the bark and boiling it, then using the resulting liquid to drip into Bors' mouth. He followed the instructions that had been drilled into him about willow bark.

Once that was done, he sat back and watched Bors. The larger man's chest rose and fell unsteadily. The bandages were cleaned as best he could, using some of his own uniform to help create new ones. He did not like being this helpless.

One thing he did not do was dwell on what Al'Kara had said while she was talking to him. He had to worry about that later. *Get Bors back to a bit of health, get him to the village, cross the bridge about Al'Kara being in league with the witch later.*

It was a long night of little rest and more worry.

Rick snapped awake to see Bors sitting up. The barbarian moved with great caution as if he was in pain. *Course he's in pain, stupid. He had a spear in his chest half a day ago.*

"Friend Rick, what is wrong?" Bors asked, his voice thick as he looked at Rick with concern.

"You were injured. I had no idea how to help you," looking down.

Bors let out a weak laugh, which dissolved into a cough. "The *Hidden Mountain* tribe is strong. I will heal. Do not worry. The medicine you made for me is helping."

"How do you—"

"There was a part of me that was listening," Bors said though he didn't look Rick in the eyes. "I don't like the fact you spoke to the witch. She has some control over your loved one, doesn't she?"

Rick pursed his lips. "Something like that," Rick muttered, again avoiding the barbarian's eyes.

Bors shook his head. "I'm sure she'll be released from whatever curse the *witch* has laid upon her. With the help of this," Bors said, thumb pointing at the black-pitted sword beside him. He looked like he wanted to reach out for it, but Rick saw a pause as if the barbarian didn't wish to take the sword up.

"What is wrong?" Rick asked.

There was a moment of silence. "A burden that I do not wish to carry forever," Bors said, his mouth quirking into a frown. Rick saw that the bigger man had a sudden look of haggardness.

"Why take it up?"

"Duty. Heavier than a mountain," there was a twist of his lip as if he told some joke.

"Then—"

Bors' fingers wrapped around the worn, leather hilt, a rictus of pain coming and going so fast, Rick wasn't sure he'd seen it. "I must, friend Rick. I am the only one who can wield her and live."

Rick looked at the barbarian askew. "What do you mean?"

Bors gave a heavy sigh. "The *Soul of the Mother* is my tribes' greatest accomplishment and greatest shame. It holds the soul of a mountain. *The Mountain* to which my tribe has dedicated its name.

"What mountain?" Rick asked, intrigued by the barbarian's anti-quated belief.

"Olympus Mons."

"Your sword holds what?"

"You heard me. The Soul of Olympus Mons, the greatest mountain of Sol. *The Soul of the Mother.*" Every word Bors spoke was with such reverence and gravitas that Rick was sure Bors *believed* it.

Rick tried not to laugh, yet he did let out a small chuckle before stifling it when Bors cut him a hard, dark look. "Bors. You are saying that Olympus Mons has a *soul*? That doesn't—"

"She did when she disappeared," Bors said as he stood, testing his limbs.

Rick was struck silent for a moment. "Wait, *Olympus Mons* disappeared? When?" He asked, unable to make sense of Bors' words.

Bors shrugged his shoulders. "I cannot tell. It was a very long time ago." He looked at Rick. "It is said she could no longer handle the burden of holding up the world."

Rick felt off for a moment. *Something doesn't add up.* "Bors. I don't know how to tell you this, but in my time, the mountain is still there. I was on Mars recently, and it was *still* there." Rick wasn't lying, per se. He hadn't seen it with the naked eye, but his instruments hadn't made any mention of a missing mountain. He had had to cut his patrol of Mars short when he found Al'Kara and had to leave the planet sooner than he thought.

"It could have been after your time, friend Rick," Bors said with a small knowing smile.

"How?" Rick asked, genuinely confused. "You come from a time when men used swords and fight green-skinned Martians—they are extinct. And the Golgoro are—"

Bors shook his head and held a hand up to stop Rick from continuing. "You do not know for a fact when you come from, right, friend Rick?"

"You do?" Rick shot back.

"No, not at all. But I have seen and witnessed many strange things that you would not believe without seeing them yourself, friend Rick."

Rick watched as, throughout the conversation, Bors seemed to grow more and more steady. The large barbarian took a stab at the air, and although he did sway a little in his fighting stance, he was able to recover himself with ease. "Bors, you aren't—"

"We should continue our journey," Bors said, settling the sword into its sheath on his back.

Rick looked at Bors, wanting to ask one more time. "Are you—"

"Yes, friend Rick," Bors interrupted, though it was through strained teeth. "Let us depart and find this village and then the witch."

Rick licked suddenly dry lips. *How much* had *Bors heard last night*? Rick wondered. Is that sword truly what he says it is? There was a part of Rick that felt that the barbarian was wrong and suffered from some tribal myth that had been passed down from one group of people to the next. In addition, although Bors' sword looked ready to fall apart, he'd seen it do some truly nasty things. Which left him with a single question: *How can an entire mountain disappear?*

The two made an odd pair. Half the time, Rick helped Bors move along the same path through the jungle. The other half, Bors moved with a bit more speed than Rick could handle and would stride ahead of the Space Ranger, calling for Rick to catch up.

They came to a small clearing and stopped for a small meal. Though Rick wanted to move faster, he knew he'd be useless in helping Al'Kara if he didn't eat and rest.

"There should be a village up ahead," Bors said after munching on the small bit of cracker bread that Rick was able to keep dry from the river.

"How do you know?" Rick asked.

"There are more tracks of the Callistians around on the trail we follow. The path is turning into a road, growing more compact, and will grow firmer as we get closer to this settlement."

CHAPTER TWENTY-THREE

And find one they did. It was a simple collection of huts that looked to be unused. As Rick strode off towards one hut, thinking he saw a hint of movement, Bors stayed where he was. So it was that Rick was caught off-guard as Bors called out and started his song while being attacked by a plethora of the bestial Callistians.

Rick watched as Bors, even as feverish as he was, let out a bellowing roar and charged the group of salivating creatures. His black sword hewed through one after another like a scythe cutting down chaffs of wheat. Rick had taken up a defensive position behind a hut that Bors stood before—protecting Rick's flank. Rick realized how stupid he had been and started shooting at any of the Callistians that came close to him or tried to attack Bors. His Tellic was flashing green death again and again as Bors tried to keep those that harried the flanks of the hut that Rick couldn't get a clear bead on with his weapon.

With a flash of red, Rick spotted the forms of Al'Kara and another of the Golgoro who stood beside her. The one besides Al'Kara held a long, silver-gleaming staff with metal bangles and flaring lights coming off it. *That is the witch?* Rick thought. They appeared in a flare of red and purple light. Blinking back tears, Rick called out for her, "Al'Kara!"

She turned, her eyes looking at him blankly. She was not dressed as he had known her; her hair was now woven into a complex braid with gems, body cloaked in a sheer gauze-like dress of green and purple. She gestured towards him. Rick was flung backward hard against the wall of the hut by some force. Rick didn't think she was *that* powerful with her Mind-Blade powers, once he rebounded off the back wall of the hut, the wind driven from his lungs by what had happened. Stunned, Rick tried to pick himself up and found it difficult. Something started to swim through his head, a strange song of some kind. It had a low, constant drumbeat just on the edge of hearing, rhythmic clapping, and low wailing. It faded in and out as he struggled to stand up.

"Let me help you, Ranger," a voice whispered in his head, the song growing more intense.

He looked around. "Who's talking?" He gasped out. At first, he thought it was Al'Kara, but it didn't make sense for her to do so. She called him *beloved.*

"I can help you with all of them. Let me in," the voice was deep and sepulchral, yet feminine.

"Who are you?" Rick fairly screamed when he got the air back in his lungs.

"I am the Soul of the Mother," the voice said, pleased with itself.

Rick slashed at the air with his Tellic. "No. I know what you do to my friend, Bors. Get out of my head."

"Even if you die here?"

Rick smirked, "Then I die free."

There was a growl of frustration in his head. There was movement at the doorway, and Rick saw the form of the other Golgoro woman staring down at him with violet eyes. She was covered in two strips of metal-trimmed cloth, yet so transparent that they were see-through. "You speak as if you have a choice in this matter?"

Rick jerked his Tellic up, firing at her. His green beam shot right through her. He shook his head as she loomed to his right. "What—"

"You have no idea what is going on, Ranger. I *am* in your head," the woman laughed. "Soon, you'll be the pawn of La'Haja... like your beloved, Al'Kara."

"Then, you should know I won't give up," Rick said. "And she *will* be free."

There was a growling sound of disgust from her. "You will die, as I will take my cousin from you, completely."

There was a moment of rage when she said those words. He could see everything filtered through a red mist for a moment. She was three feet to the left of where he thought she was. He jerked his arm that way and fired several times without aiming.

One ray struck her in the arm, causing the red mist to fade. La'Haja crumpled to the ground while gripping the stump of her left arm with her right. She screamed for help. She was screaming for Al'Kara to help.

Rick pushed himself to his feet, seeing that Bors was holding his own against the Callistians, who had backed off, seeing their mistress witch had fallen. Rick moved closer to her, eyeing the staff that had fallen in the dirt beside her, with her right hand and forearm, gripping it tightly.

When he turned back, Al'Kara appeared beside the fallen La'Haja. Before Rick could speak, Al'Kara pulled her wounded cousin to her feet, gripping onto the staff, ignoring the macabre appendage.

Rick asked, "Al'Kara?"

She looked at him with her own hard eyes. "You won't understand, beloved," Al'Kara said. "This is a family matter."

The words slapped him like a physical blow. He wanted to reach her. "Please, Al'Kara... I—"

Al'Kara shook her head hard, looking away from him as La'Haja murmured something to her. Then, she pinned him with a stare, eyes filling with tears. "I love you, and I always will." The staff flared into a bright nimbus of purple light. She disappeared in the blast of light, making Rick jerk his arm up to shield his eyes.

CHAPTER TWENTY-FOUR

Rick crumpled to the ground, gripping his eyes. He still held the strange ray gun in his hand, yet it dropped to the ground as Bors moved closer, the last of the Callistians gone.

"What is wrong, Rick?"

"I can't see, Bors. That staff—"

"Let me see," Bors said. He rested a big hand on Rick's shoulder and pried a hand away from Rick's face. The big, burly hand very deftly teased open one of Rick's eyelids. He saw an eye that looked normal to him. "You will recover, my friend. You do not bear any signs of blindness."

"Still, how am I going to move?" Rick asked.

Bors sighed and toed the ray gun towards his friend. "Pick up your weapon. I will find something to bandage your eyes to help them rest."

Once he had seen to Rick's eyes and settled the Space Ranger, Bors looked from him to the mountain and tried to find a path. For the first third of the way, Bors thought he saw a trail that twisted around the mountainside in a long series of switchbacks. He knew it would take time to make a sled to drag his friend along or have him hold his shoulder, but Rick could not travel without help.

It was not that difficult to cut the needed wood for the rough litter for Rick. The Space Ranger groused about being led around like a "babe in the woods," yet he was silent when Bors pushed him onto the sled and told him to be quiet. He then turned to the beginning of the trail up the mountain, grabbed the litter, and started to pull.

He felt the weight of his arms and legs dragging at him as he constructed the sled. He knew what was going on. *Mother* had taken back the strength given to him. Still, he pushed forward, not needing it. He worked for an hour before making a litter that would suffice to drag Rick up the mountain towards the witches and their cave.

———

After several hours of travel, Rick found he could see again, of that Bors was thankful. He wasn't sure how much longer he could drag his blind friend along. With the strength depleted from *Mother,* he knew he would not make it.

"Rick, I am glad you are awake," Bors said, exhaustion shaking him after pulling them closer to a third of the way up the last switchback.

"What are we going to do?" Rick asked, looking at their position.

"We will rest here, and then we will take the rest of the mountain tomorrow and fight the two witches," Bors said, settling down on a rock that would do for a temporary seat.

Rick started at the mention of "witches." "Only one is a witch. The other is—"

"The other is the one you love," Bors asked while digging into the last of the rations Ghurd and his Callistians had sacrificed to speed him on his journey.

Rick nodded. He looked like he wanted to say more but stopped.

Bors took a deep breath as he pulled out the last of the strong alcohol. "She is evil."

Rick scowled at that. "She is *not*. I know her heart."

Bors cocked an eyebrow. "How? You have never—"

Rick settled back, pressing his head against the rock for a moment, looking up at the stars. "Let me tell you about how we first met."

Bors uncorked the jug and took a long pull of the drink. He gasped at the hideous stuff but swallowed down the liquid fire. "Proceed."

After the story, Bors nodded. "So, she loves you. What about—"

"I love her as well," Rick said. "Damn whatever rule or code says I can't. I love Al'Kara of the Golgoro, and I'll protect her life to my dying breath."

Bors tossed the bottle to Rick.

"I couldn't," Rick said. "I—"

"A simple oath keeps you from loving her, which would have broken. Can't your oath about drink be stretched?" Bors asked, smiling at his friend. "Or is your oath more important than—"

Rick took a deep swing of the stuff, and Bors bit his cheek not to laugh as Rick looked ready to spit the content out. "That's awful!"

"And, yet you are drinking it," Bors said, gesturing to the bottle. "Have a bit more."

Rick did and made a sour face.

This time, Bors did let out a laugh as the two finished the last of the noxious rotgut and had the last of their thick oatmeal cakes that Rick produced. "Get some sleep, my friend," Bors said as he finished the last of the cake. "We have the end of our journey tomorrow."

CHAPTER TWENTY-FIVE

The drink was stronger than Bors thought, for when he woke, he and Rick had the minions of the witches around them. He tried to stand yet found he couldn't. He heard the cackling laugh of one of the two green-skinned devil women of the ancient, long-dead race, the Golgoro. He saw the one named Al'Kara, Rick's beloved. He turned to see his friend was still asleep and already hoisted onto a litter and being carried away.

He was not bound but could not move, and he knew it was the powers of the witch. Her right hand had a small burn on the fingertips, and several of her minions looked as though they had burned themselves somehow, their weapons shifting into their left hands. He thought it odd. He knew *something* had burned them, as the sickly-sweet smell of scorched flesh hung in the air.

"He still loved you, witch," Bors said.

"I know. And I will always love him," Al'Kara said.

"Then, why do—"

She waved her hand. "What would a Northern Tribesman know of honor? Though I don't know what clan you are," she said.

"Hidden Mountain."

"There is no such clan."

Bors smirked. "And, there is no Golgoro for my tribe. You had all died an eon ago before The Mountain went into hiding."

Al'Kara gave him a raised eyebrow. "How can The Mountain go missing?" She asked, somehow knowing he meant Olympus Mons.

"I don't know, but she still lives in our hearts, and with her power, I will defeat you and your cousin."

"If it were up to me, I would kill you now, native scum," Al'Kara said with a sneer. She quirked her hand, and Bors was lifted and carried to the edge of the trail. He looked down, seeing the long drop.

"But, your cousin has need of me?"

"Your sword. None of these minions can take it. Nor can I seem to touch it," she said, giving him a sneer.

Bors saw something in her eyes when she spoke about not being able to touch the *Soul of the Mother. She is afraid*, Bors thought. "Then, you should take me to see your cousin."

"Or I drop you and get the sword from your mangled corpse. That could be the reason I can't touch it, being bound to you."

"Are you willing to take that chance?" Bors asked, a smirk still on his lips.

"Al'Kara, you are better than this!" Rick shouted, waking up and calling out.

"Beloved, please stop," she said, gesturing towards Rick, and he stopped making sounds. He looked like he tried to scream, yet nothing was coming out, no sound whatsoever.

Bors and Rick were borne up the mountain towards the large skull top. Yet, before they reached the giant open mouth, the group of Callistians and the witch stopped and entered a secret doorway that led into a metal-framed corridor. The walls were a shiny metal, tinged a light blue, the floor looked to be made of marble, yet when he was able to walk, Bors found it to be cool tile.

The two were then brought to the throne room of the witch, La'Haja. Bors knew that Witch Al'Kara was under some spell or compulsion that made her help this other devilish Golgoro. He knew that if he had to, he would kill them both.

On a black, stone throne, sat La'Haja, her smile cold; her eyes shone with the light of the staff she held in her right hand. Bors balked at seeing her with both limbs, having seen Rick's ray gun sever one. The new arm was metallic and gleamed in the lights of the various globes of light that hung in the air above the throne in the large throne room.

La'Haja moved forward on the throne, "Bring the barbarian to me," she said.

Al'Kara did as asked, keeping Bors from fully touching the floor except for his toes of his hobnail boots that scraped along the tile of the throne room. La'Haja made a fist, and Bors dropped to his knees. He heard the other witch gasp and take several steps back. Then, Al'Kara muttered, "I will see to my *beloved* then," and her footsteps faded behind Bors.

"Do you think you can kill me?" La'Haja asked with a smirk.

"Yes," he said.

"How so?" La'Haja asked, an eyebrow quirking. She raised a hand, and two dozen of her guards formed a loose ring around him, these Callistians even larger than the others. A strange miasma exuded from them. Bors' nose wrinkled at the horrid aroma.

"The *Soul of the Mother* will lend me the strength I need," Bors said, standing up. He reached for the sword.

La'Haja shot a hand out, and Bors felt his arm lock up, his fingers close enough to scrape the leather wrapping, yet not enough to grip it.

"You are a fool," La'Haja said. "You are going to die, and that sword will give me what I need."

"She will never bow to you."

"Don't be too sure," La'Haja said.

A shimmering ghost of the Mother appeared at Bors' elbow. "My bearer, you are risking yourself far more than you need to."

"It is needed," Bors said mentally. "I have a mission to complete."

"I am telling you to back down," the Mother said, lightly touching his left arm. "Please. Stop resisting."

Bors' eyes bulged for a second, and he looked down. Her hands were pale, as was the rest of her face. He looked at the illusion for half a second and then snapped his head back to La'Haja. "You are a fool," he said and, with all his might, shoved his hand closer to the hilt of his sword.

The moment his palm touched the sword, the song of the sword filled his head, and he was free. He drew the giant sword like it was made of paper, swinging it down to bisect one of the guardian Callistians in a single cut. He felt his body fully give into the song as he whirled around to meet another guard with a long metal pike. And, above it all, was the scream of rage from La'Haja.

He lost himself in the song until he was grappled by something. His arms were unable to move, and his body felt as though it was held by a giant hand. He turned to see Al'Kara moving closer and closer, but he also saw Rick running towards his woman. He grabbed her and whirled her around, pulling her into a kiss.

Bors didn't have time to understand what was going on, losing track of his friend as the mind-controlled Callistians surged around him, their nails tipped with small blades glinting in the strange hanging globe lights of the throne room. Their faces were devoid of thought, only rictuses of anger on bestial faces to show fangs drooling with venomous saliva. They only wished to do violence against Bors.

Taking a deep breath, he calmed his mind and felt the rage of *Soul of the Mother* out of reach. *Mother, I need—*

Oh, you need my help, my bearer? I thought—

I die, you are left here. Is that what you want... Mother? Bors silenced her with that question.

His body moved automatically, dodging and blocking the worst of the swipes of the creatures as *Mother* hemmed and hawed, refusing to answer. He felt his lips stretch into a rictus of a snarl as he flung himself towards the creatures. "Bors of the Hidden Mountain *will not* die today! *With* or *without* your help, woman!" He shouted, opening his eyes.

The voice wasn't his. He felt the ecstatic joy of the fight flow over him, the smell of blood being spilled in battle, causing the same *thrum* of rage to surge through him anew. He felt the rage boiling over from

Mother, sweeping him away with the mindlessness of combat. Lost in the fight, he sang of the Hidden Mountain of his people. Of the *Soul of the Mother*.

And it was good.

Rick sprinted past the insane Callistians—though their fury was focused on Bors. One of them caught sight of Rick running and swung a clumsy arm towards him. Rick slipped under the last guard's weak attack. The guard turned too late as Rick shot him in the back. Rick didn't stop to think of what he did; he needed to get to Al'Kara. *Find her. Focus on that!*

He saw her moving into the throne room, her arms raised. She saw Bors in a whirl of motion then stopped as Al'Kara's powers ensnared him. Bors could see Al'Kara and Rick as he sprinted towards his love. Without pausing, he grabbed her, spun her around, and kissed her. "Al'Kara of the Golgoro, I love you."

A look of joy spread over her face, then complete confusion. "Beloved, what... what is going on?" She asked Rick, looking around confused beyond measure.

"You tell me!" Rick said, grabbing ahold of Al'Kara arm. He pulled her close, "I thought I'd lost you."

There was a blast of purple light, and a form loomed behind Al'Kara. La'Haja emerged, screaming, "You have!" La'Haja was lunging forward with her sparking staff, swinging towards Rick's head.

Al'Kara wheeled around when her cousin spoke. "Cousin, what is the meaning of this? You said—"

The staff stopped with a gesture from Al'Kara. She lashed out with her other hand, trying to stab at La'Haja with her blue-tinged mind-blade. Rick took a step back as the two fought, looking for a way to get a clean shot off. He held back, not wanting to hurt Al'Kara.

La'Haja laughed, slapping away her cousin's attack. She dropped the staff, and the metal staff hovered at her side, floating within reach at all times as she moved. "You are a banished psi-blade. I thought I

could use your powers, but you can't be *trusted*. Not with *him* around."
She gestured at Rick, and his body went rigid. *"You've* been a thorn in
my side *far* too long, Rick Tavish. I will *finally* be able to do something I have wanted to do for far too long."

Rick looked at the Golgoro woman, confused. "I've never laid eyes
on you before."

She smirked. "Nor shall you ever!" Her hand clenched, fingers bent
as if clutching something in a tight grip.

Rick felt a pain pierce his chest as if his lungs were being stabbed
from the inside. He felt wet coughs rack his body. He felt bloody spittle
and phlegm fly from his mouth and paint his lips and the tile floor.
Something wet oozed over his chin as he tried to draw a breath. He
looked at La'Haja, trying to speak. Nothing came out except a ragged
croak. He staggered and swayed as he continued to cough. Pain
wracked his body.

There was a sudden flare from his Tellic to his left, and La'Haja
crumpled. Rick looked at the ruined body. He turned weakly to see
Al'Kara holding his Tellic, her hand soaked in blood, *his blood. How?*
How could—

"Your blood, beloved." She said, kneeling down next to him. "We
need to go." She pulled an arm over her shoulder. "We have to get to
the portal and get out of here."

"What about Bors?"

Al'Kara turned to see the barbarian raging, cutting down the Callistian guards like wheat. "He will survive. La'Haja is gone. We need to
get you to a place where you can be healed."

Together, the two limped towards the doorway towards which
Al'Kara gestured. Beyond, he saw the glowing blue and gold of the
portal that had brought the two of them to Callisto. He didn't want to
go, yet he had to seek medical treatment. The witch was dead, and
Bors would be able to survive.

Bors found himself alone for a moment, the guards were cowering as
La'Haja was cut down. He saw her crumple to nothing and was ready

to fall to his knees when the ground shook, and the throne hummed to life, giving off a dark purple hum. The seat of the throne separated, and from it emerged La'Haja. She settled onto the seat, scowling. She screamed out, "My cousin betrayed me! Only steel will do my bidding," and a large metal humanoid emerged from behind the throne.

Bors charged at the thing yet jerked to one side as the arm leveled at him, and a bolt of green light shot towards him. Only his quick movement kept him from being hit. He hid behind one of the pillars of the throne room. He peeked around the corner and jerked his head back as another bolt of green burned through the first two inches of the thick stone column.

"Do not ruin my throne room! Kill him with your own claws!" La'Haja shouted.

Bors twisted towards the other side of the column and sprinted towards the throne. He had not heard the movement of the robot yet turned to see the thing had moved forward and grabbed him, fighting for the sword. Bors pushed his arms forward, trying to shove the robot away, yet the thing clung to him. Then, its clawed hand reached up to grab at the pitted blade.

The robot and Bors were knocked to the tile floor by an explosion of air and blue light. Bors found himself on his feet, looking at an armless robot trying to get up. La'Haja screamed at the robot to get up. She continued as Bors slammed the sword to the hilt in the robot's chest and ripped upwards, letting out a feral yell. The thing sparked and jerked and was still a moment later.

When he turned toward La'Haja, she was alone, curled up on the throne, tears in her eyes. "All of them betray me in the end."

"You are a witch! It is your lot to be betrayed," Bors said while striding towards her. "You may cry and try to ensorcell me, yet I will—"

"I don't care anymore, Bors. My *people* will die. I wanted to help, but it can't be helped." She sat down on the throne. "I give up. I am so tired. There is no reason to go on." Her body slumped in the throne. Bors watched as her body shrank in upon herself, growing more and more withered.

When he reached the throne, he found a desiccated corpse. "Your people will die. I know, for in my time, they are but a memory."

There was a dry laugh from the corpse as it lifted its toothless skeletal face towards Bors, eyes turning to dust, the tongue a dried husk of a wiggling worm. "Don't worry, Bors, you have carried out your task. I am dead and will never hurt the Callistians again."

Bors snorted at the witch and slammed his sword into the center of the corpse. There was a loud keening that came from both the sword and the thing in the throne, and then he was rocked on his heels by the shuddering of his sword. On the throne, there was now nothing, not even dust—only a black, charred form from where La'Haja the witch had sat a moment before.

Bors felt his rage quelled and silent. All around him was death. The altered Callistians had been slaughtered. He fell to his knees, feeling *Mother's* hands on his shoulders as he came out of his rage. He didn't speak; he could barely breathe, as his body was past any complaint. He watched as *Mother* consumed the Callistians in her macabre ritual, their blood turning into a purplish-black haze around Bors. He turned his head to see a glowing portal of purple and green wink out as Rick and one of the witches ran through it. Yet the other witch, La'Haja, was dead and dust.

"The witch is dead," he said, smiling. It *hurt* to smile, yet he had completed the quest he'd set out to accomplish. He hoped that Rick and the other witch had survived, but he wasn't sure what would happen to them. Al'Kara had been a witch who helped in the end in the Times before. It had not been the strangest thing he had experienced. Names are strange, he thought.

The witch is dead, Mother whispered in his head. *Rest now, my bearer.*

Bors dropped his head, waiting for *Mother* to finish her feeding. "Yes, rest sounds wonderful. Only a few moments, though." He nodded off as *Mother* finished her macabre ritual, unconscious and dreaming of more pleasant things. His last thoughts were of the Callistians and his new quest to somehow get back to Mars.

TO BE CONTINUED...
IN
IRONMONGERS

ABOUT THE AUTHOR

Lon E. Varnadore is an awarding winning science fiction author. This is the first omnibus of the Known World Series.

ALSO BY LON E. VARNADORE

Mostly Human The first of the 4Pollack series, a noir science fiction novel.

Junker Blues: Mars To control him, they filled his veins with tech. To escape their grasp, he'll risk certain death.

CPSIA information can be obtained
at www.ICGtesting.com
Printed in the USA
BVHW042115180922
647356BV00003B/128